WHERE THE MUSIC WAS

Where
the
Music
Was

FIFTEEN STORIES BY

Charles East

HARCOURT, BRACE & WORLD, INC.
NEW YORK

Some of these stories first appeared
in the pages of *The Antioch Review,*
Mademoiselle,
The Virginia Quarterly Review,
and *The Yale Review.*
For permission to reprint them here,
the author is grateful.

For Sarah and Charlie

The centaur rides down Beale Street
In a Cadillac sedan
And four white colts go frolicking
Across the gravid land.

        And I have known
The anonymity of towns at night
When the harsh blood was calm a moment, losing
The weary flooding motion of this love.

—GEORGE MARION O'DONNELL

CONTENTS

WHERE THE MUSIC WAS

Fisherman's Wife

It was in the spring of the year that Ada noticed something wrong. The river was high and the sky was overcast. Any afternoon she could see the water from the house and she could see Jimson by the river bluffs, his shoulders hunched into the wind, walking there. His back was to her; he watched the far bank, the bar to the north, and to the south the mud flat where the willows grew. The spring before, the spring before that, he would have been busy with his lines and nets, mending traps, caulking his boats. He built his own boats, painted them himself, named them pretty names like the *Beulah* and the *Wandering Jew*. And one he called the *Ada Dee*. Spring was a busy time of year. The

3

smell of tar was in the air, and Jimson came in tired and slept hard. But not this spring. This spring his back was to her; he watched the far bank. Maybe it's the boy he's thinking of, she told herself. Maybe blaming himself. If he hadn't let the boy go work on the dredges . . . Once he said that. And she said, "You couldn't've stopped him nohow." Nobody could. The boy had a mind of his own —got that from Jimson. He went off and worked on the dredges, and one day up near Talahaw, trying to clear a line, he slipped.

He came up once, they said. He came up and he tried to swim, but the current there was strong. He went back under. And Jimson went up to Talahaw to help them look for him. For most of a week he was gone, and all that time she waited in the little house that they had lived in first. She could see it through the window there, beyond the berry bushes and this side of the bluffs where Jimson walked. He had brought her downriver from Cairo in a skiff and he had built that house for her. It was one room and it was built high, so you could see the coal barges and the sternwheelers, and when Jimson was out running his nets, out in the channel there, she could see him, too. But after the boy was born he built this other house—three rooms and a porch, and screens for the windows and a tin roof for the rain to beat against. Now the screens were out and the roof was dull with rust.

So she watched Jimson walking by the bluffs, and she wondered what it was that bothered him. Something I done, she thought. Not been good to him. But I been as good as I knew how, she thought—come way off down here with him, looked after him, let him when he wanted to. Only now he never wanted to. "What's the matter?" she said. "Nothing," he said. "Something," she said. And then he took to going into town. Not often. Maybe once a week. One night he didn't come home at all, and when she asked him why, he wouldn't say, just turned his back on her. Then she knew. It was as if she had known a long time, and in a way she was glad. It was nothing I done, she thought.

One morning he went out and walked and he came back in again. He changed his clothes. "Where you going?" she said. "In town?"

He stood there, his shoulders hunched, looking out the door. In a minute he said, "I'm liable to be gone a day or two."

"That long?" she said.

"You need anything?"

"No," she said.

He kept standing there. There was something on his mind. "Ada Dee," he said, "if I was to . . ." He turned. "If I was to bring somebody back with me . . ."

She looked at him.

"You know what I mean?"

Maybe so, she thought.

"A man . . ."

A man needs somebody young, she thought. She was younger than him once. She was younger than him when he brought her down from Cairo in a skiff.

"He can't help himself."

She didn't let on that she heard. Maybe she didn't.

"You going to be here when I get back?" he said.

She started to say, "I always am, ain't I?"

"You going to be here?"

She nodded.

That was all he said. He picked up his hat from off the chair and went out the door and down the steps and got in the pickup. Ada stood there watching him. The last she saw of him he was headed up the levee side, going fast, and he blew the horn to signal his good-by.

He was gone three days, and two of those it rained. On the second day, in the rain, she moved. She got some of her things together and carried them down the path through the berry bushes to the other house. She swept it out and made the bed and she built a fire in the grate to take the dampness out, for the April wind was cold. During the night the rain stopped and in the morning the sky was blue. She got the rest of her things and carried them down the path to the house. Then she fell across the bed, and for the first time since Jimson left she slept without remembering.

She awoke hearing her name called. It was Jimson's voice. She went to the door and opened it.

"I been calling you and calling you," he said, coming down the path.

"I was asleep," she said. Her eyes burned.

"What you doing down here?"

"I come down here yesterday," she said. She knew he had looked for her.

"Come up to the house," he said. "I want you to meet somebody."

Behind him, on the steps of the other house, she saw the girl, saw her hair, yellow in the sun. "In a minute," she said. She went and combed her hair, hunted for a mirror she could look into. She found a piece of one. But she could only see her eyes. Her brother Fred used to say she had the bluest eyes. Well, not any more, she thought: the river fades blue eyes. She cocked her head. She held the mirror out from her. She could almost see her face in it.

"You coming?" Jimson called. He was by the steps still. She went outside and up the path with him. Neither of them spoke until they reached the other house. Ada walked

6

slow. Sometimes he got ahead of her. "I called you and called you," he said.

"Did you?" she said.

They went up the steps. The girl was on the porch.

"This here's Eddris," Jimson said.

The girl smiled timidly. "Hidy-do," she said.

"Eddris?"

"Yes, mam," the girl said.

Ada looked at her. "You're pretty," she said. "You got pretty hair, and I see your feet are little."

"Thank you, mam."

She turned to say something to Jimson, something about a girl ought to have little feet, but Jimson was gone. She saw him going down the steps. "Eddris," she said again. "That's a pretty name." And she thought: he'll name a boat for her.

"I never liked it," the girl said.

"You didn't? You know how Jimson got his name?" Ada waited until she shook her head. "His daddy was named Jim and they got to calling him Jim's son. Jimson. You know how they call people."

The two of them stood there.

"Don't you want a peach?" the girl said.

"No, thank you," Ada said.

"We bought a bushel at a place up near Rena Lara."

"This time of year?"

The girl nodded. "Must've brought them in from Florida."

"You live up near Rena Lara?"

"No, mam. I come from out the other side of Pace. My daddy . . . you may know him. Lige Moore. He used to farm the old Grimmett place."

"Oh, yes," Ada said.

"I was born out there."

"You're mighty young," Ada said.

"Yes, mam."

"When I come here . . ." She saw Jimson out among his nets. "I was no older than you. The river was . . ." She pointed. "Way out yonder where you see those stobs. You see those stobs?"

The girl nodded.

"It was way out there. You see where it's cut away at the bluffs? One day it'll run right under us. You wouldn't think so, would you?"

The girl shook her head. She was looking out toward the river.

"Only I don't guess we'll be here then."

"When?" the girl said.

"When the river's where we are."

"I mean, how long you guess . . . ?"

"Oh," she said. "I don't know. Maybe a hundred years." Or a night, she thought. She remembered the dream. There was nothing here. She was standing on the levee and there was nothing here, not even this house. Just the river. And she remembered the night Jimson came back from Tala-haw. *You didn't find him?* she said. And he said, *No.* And she said, *I want my boy.* And he said, *He won't never come up, Ada Dee. He's down there in one of them eddies and he won't never come up.* And she said, *Never?* And he said, *Never.* "Well, I got to be getting back . . ." she said.

The girl looked at her.

"You need anything?"

"No, mam."

"Well, if you do . . ."

"I wish you'd take some of these peaches," the girl said.

Ada shook her head. She's wanting me to take something, she thought, and I'm wanting her to take something. She stood there on the steps and she could see Jimson looking up at her. She was almost to the path when she heard him call to her to wait. She stopped.

"I like to forgot this," he said. It was black and it was shaped like a hatbox. He lifted it out of the back of the pickup.

"What?" she said.

He set it on the ground. "Open it."

"You," she said.

He stooped and opened it.

"A Victrola," she said.

"I got you some records, too," he said.

She ran her fingers across the bright green felt on the turntable, saw her face, and then his, caught in the nickel-plated arm. "Give it to her," she said.

"I got it for you," he said. "You always wanted one."

"I know I did."

"Well, it's yours."

Over his shoulder she saw the girl standing on the porch. "No," she said. "Give it to her." She started to say, "It gets lonesome here." But Jimson never knew what lonesome was.

He closed the top to the Victrola and picked it up, stood there in the path.

"Anyway," she said, "I wouldn't have time to play it."

He looked at her. "When I got back here and didn't find you . . ." he said. He kept looking at her. "I thought you'd gone someplace."

"Where?"

"I don't know."

One day I guess I will, she thought.

It was a bright moonlight night. The way Ada lay she could lift herself and look out of the window toward the other house. She could see the light in the back room and she could hear the Victrola music, quick-step music she lost the time to, and then there would be a spell of quiet before the music started in again. The land was lit by moonlight as far as she could see. There was the house, and there were the nets, and the cottonwoods, and behind her, if she looked, the river bluffs. She knew how the river looked at night when the moon was out and the clouds were scudding across the sky, how the water lapped against the bar, how the bar was warm in the moonlight, and how toward dawn it cooled. How white it was. How lonesome, too.

"Here's where we'll sleep tonight," Jimson had said. He caught the skiff and pulled it up the bar. Then he took the blanket out and spread it on the sand, and he pulled her down beside him there. But the moon was in her eyes, and the sound of water lapping in her ears. She began to cry.

"What's the matter?" he said. "You scared?"

"A little," she said.

"There's nothing to be scared of." He caught her hand. "You sorry you come away with me?"

"No," she said.

"Want me to take you back?"

She shook her head.

"You sure?"

"I couldn't go back now," she said, "even if I wanted to."

"Wonder what your papa said—you running off with me."

A Shanks, she thought. *I hear you been runnin' around with one of them Shanks*, her papa said. And she said, *Just because* . . . And he said, *You gonna end up with one of them towheaded babies, livin' back of the levee. You ever hear of a Shanks that amounted to nothin'?* "Plenty," she said.

Jimson smiled.

"How far we come?" she asked. They had lost sight of Cairo just as the sun came up.

"A good way," he said.

"How far we got to go?"

"Three . . . four days," he said. "We'll follow the river down, and we'll look for us a place."

"What is it about the river?" she said.

"What?" he said.

"A Shanks can't leave the river . . ."

"No," he said, "it's in his blood, I guess."

Ada thought of Jimson, the river bar and the moonlight, and of those she left behind: her papa and her brother Fred, her Aunt Della, the one-legged man her aunt was married to. He liked his liquor. Her papa did too. He'd get drunk and he'd come home cussing, saying things he didn't mean. Only Fred said he did. *That old man,* he said. *One day that old man* . . . And the boy. It was strange now how she thought of him, like somebody she had never known, or had known but forgotten. A face. Not even a face. Like the touch of wind or the sound of water on a bar. If they had found him, she thought, if there was someplace I could go to . . . take some flowers to . . . a place the other side of the levee . . . but the river . . .

In the distance she heard the Victrola music and the sound of laughter, a young girl's laughter. She lifted herself on her elbows and looked out of the window toward the other house. The moon was bright. It inched its way across the sky, across her window and the sill, and when it touched her arm she drew back, pulled her arm away, for the touch of it was cold.

That night Ada had a dream. She was standing on the levee. She had stood there in her other dreams. And this house . . . the other house . . . there was nothing here. Just the river. She wondered where Jimson was. She had waited so long. And suddenly she knew what she was waiting for, what she had always waited for, and she came awake and cried out, "No!" I ought to tell him, she thought, and she got into her clothes and started up the path to the other house. But there in the moonlight she stopped. He'd only laugh at me, she thought.

When she awoke in the morning Jimson was out caulking his boats. The other mornings he was up early, and he was out late into the afternoons. She watched him from her window there, and sometimes when she watched the girl was beside him or behind him, but close to him, or running to the house to bring him things. He worked hard and when the men from town came to rent his boats, his boats were ready, and when the river dropped, his nets were tarred and his boxes strong enough to hold the fish that he would catch. I'll tell him yet, she thought.

Ada had never found time before; she had been kept busy doing things. Now there was nothing to do. She got up in the morning. She went to bed at night. One day she sat down and wrote a letter to her brother Fred. She never knew where Fred was, except Cairo maybe, but she wrote him anyway, told him what she was doing, which was not much to tell, asked him what had become of him, what had become of her papa, her Aunt Della and the one-legged man her aunt was married to. *I guess all dead,* she wrote. And she wrote a P.S.: *I hope not.* The letter was returned. She folded it and put it away, and she told herself that one day she would write to the postmaster in Cairo and ask him Fred's address.

The things she needed Jimson brought. Once, sometimes twice, a week he went into town and he brought her her things first, stood at the steps and called to her, and when she answered came inside. "You all right?" he would say.

"I'm all right," she would say.

"You need anything?"

She would shake her head.

"That chimney," he said once. "It needs fixing. I got to fix it before winter comes." And he looked at her like he remembered how cold it got there in the little house they lived in first.

She wanted to say, "I had a dream . . ."

But he said, "You don't never come up to the house."

"No," she said.

"Why not?"

"Oh," she said, "I get busy . . ."

One evening when she came out to get a breath of air he was standing in the path. He had stood there other times like that. "Hot," she said.

"Yeah," he said.

"It's lightning. Maybe we'll get some rain."

He kept standing there. In a little while he came and sat down on the steps by her. Neither of them spoke. They just sat there, the way they used to sit. Sometimes they wouldn't say anything for an hour or more, and it would rain, or the baby would cry, or the mosquitoes would get so bad they had to go inside. And she thought: what if I had never come off down here with him? *You gonna end up with one of them towheaded babies,* her papa had said, *livin' back of the levee . . .* And she thought: if I had it all to do again . . .

The girl on the porch was calling him.

"All right," he called. He got up. "Well," he said, "I guess I got to be going . . ."

"Jimson . . ."

He turned and looked at her.

"Be careful," she said.

"What you mean?"

"I mean, be careful."

He laughed. "Ada Dee . . ."

"When you go out on the river," she said. And she knew it didn't matter. She had told him but it didn't matter.

That was in July.

One August noon two of the men who came to rent the boats brought the word. They came skimming across the water to the landing out of sight and up the bluffs between the cottonwoods. They brought the word to the girl, and Ada heard her holler. She heard her holler and she went up the path through the berry bushes to the other house. It's over, she thought. She didn't even ask; she knew.

The men told her. Jimson was pulling in a net, out in the channel there, and he fell out of the boat and went under and never came up. They figured he got tangled in the net, and they hauled it in, but they never found a sign of him. He never came up, so they figured maybe an eddy took him under, spun him around and held him there, close to the bottom in the undertow.

The men told her; then they left to go for help. They went to get the men and the hooks, to grapple in the river until the sun went down. Ada tried to talk to the girl, tried to tell her things. "You're young," she said. "Sooner or later . . ." But the girl cried harder, and after a while Ada walked away. She walked down the steps, and the sun was bright, and she stood there listening. Nobody called her. Nobody said, "Ada Dee." She went and got her things and put them in a cardboard box. She changed her dress. Then she tucked the box under her arm and went out the door and up the path, past the house, and up the road toward the levee and the other side. She heard somebody calling her. She looked back. The girl was on the porch, calling her to stay, but she had told the girl all there was to tell, and the road ahead was long. She reached the top of the levee and saw the world from there, the fields and the grove of mock orange trees, and she went down again, to the cattle gap and across it to the gravel road beyond. She walked slower now, for the river was out of sight. And as she walked the men came in the pickup trucks. The truck in back stopped, and the men who had gone for help called out to her, "Mrs. Shanks . . ."

She turned and looked at them.

"Have they found him yet?"

She shook her head. The dust blew over her.

"We got to get on up there and start looking if we're going to find him by sundown."

"You're not going to," she said.

The men looked at her. "How come?"

"They never do," she said.

They tipped their hats. The truck started up. A voice in motion called to her, "Where you going?"

"Cairo," she said.

A
Sunday
Drive

"The children are here."

Miss Odell stirred. For a moment she forgot where she was. There was only the fig tree outside the window and the fern in the pot and the bed painted white, and she thought, Where did I come from? Who brought me here? And then the woman spoke again and said, "The children are here," and all she said was, "Oh." I better get up and dress, she thought, and she remembered that she *was* dressed. The woman had dressed her and told her she could lie down for a few minutes until the children came, and she said, "What day is this?" And the woman said, "Sunday," primping her hair.

She liked the other woman best. The other woman brought her rock candy and swapped her pillow for the one she said was hard, and when she cried the other woman didn't ask her why, or tell her to stop. *You go ahead and cry, Miss Ode,* she said. *You cry and you'll feel better.*

One day, she knew, she would remember where she had come from; it would all come back to her and leave her dizzy, like a deep breath of air. There had been another place. The fern in the pot had come from there; whoever brought her here had brought the fern, and the women had watered it, and they said, *Your fern is growing so,* and she knew it was her fern. It was all they brought with her.

"You don't want to make the children wait," the woman said. And she said, "What children?" And the woman said, "Mr. Kincaid and his wife." And she thought, I don't know any Mr. Kincaid. Maybe one of Sister Maggie's sons. Or one of Tete's boys. Was it a Kincaid Tete married? I'll ask them, she thought.

"Which of the children are you?" she asked. And the boy said, "This is Bubba, Aunt Ode." And she said, "Oh, yes." "And here's Polly to see you too, Aunt Ode," he said. And she said, "Polly," and remembered Tete married a Dunn. "Where you children been?" she asked. She always asked that, and they always said, "I declare, it looked like we weren't ever going to get over here to see you, Aunt Ode."

"How long can we keep her out?" the girl said. And the woman said, "You don't want to tire her." "We're just going to take her for a Sunday drive," the boy said. "Here," he said, and he helped to get her in the car, "you sit up here with me, Aunt Ode. Where would you like to ride today?"

"Oh," she said, "it don't make a bit of difference."

"Maybe to the cemetery," the girl said.

"No," Miss Odell said quickly, "I don't want to go to the cemetery." They had taken her to the cemetery once,

17

and the girl had some flowers, and she said, *Aunt Ode, we brought some roses for you to put on Miss Vashti's grave.* And Miss Odell said, *Mama liked roses.* When was that? she thought.

She could not remember time now. She could only remember time then, and sometimes she would say to herself, *I was born Friday, April 4, 1879. I was married Monday, June 13, 1898, at 5:30 in the evening. Sister Maggie was born December 2, 1886. Mama died Wednesday, May 25, 1904, at 2:12 in the afternoon, of a bilious fever.* Sometimes she said these things aloud, and the woman heard her and said, *How you keep all those things in your head is beyond me,* and that tickled her and she laughed. She had all those things in her head, but there were so many things she had put away and never found again.

"Well, we'll just ride," the girl said, "and while we're out we'll collect your rents for you." "We're still collecting your rents for you, Aunt Ode," the boy said. And she said, "What rents?" And the boy said, "You remember your rental property." "Your nigra property," the girl said.

I never had any nigra property, Miss Odell thought. Her papa did. Her papa owned a whole lot of nigra houses, and they called it Floyd Addition. Late on summer evenings they would drive through Floyd Addition and the nigras would be on their porches and they would call out, *Good evenin', Cap'n Floyd,* and her papa would nod his head and say, *Good evenin'.* She could smell the dust and she could see the flowers in the yards, the foxgloves and the hollyhocks. But that wasn't where I *was,* she thought.

"Maybe after we collect the rent we'll stop and get you a sweet limeade," the boy said. "You know how you like sweet limeade."

"That's so," she said. Now, whose boy are you? she

thought. Sister Maggie's? No, Sister Maggie's boy wouldn't be a Kincaid. "Who was your mama?" she asked. And the boy said, "Lettie, Aunt Ode." And she said, "Maggie's Lettie." She laughed. "One time," she said, "Sister Maggie couldn't get Lettie to take turpentine for the croup. She was just a little thing. And Maggie said, 'Sugar, you got to take this.' And Lettie just closed her mouth. She wasn't going to open it. And Maggie said, 'I'll tell you what. You always admiring my amber jewelry. You take this turpentine and I'll give you my amber jewelry.'" Miss Odell laughed and the boy laughed, and he said, "That's one story Mama didn't tell me."

"Look out the window, Aunt Ode," the girl said. "You not enjoying your ride."

"Aren't the yards pretty?" she said. And the boy said, "You know where you are now, don't you?" No, she thought, I don't know where I am now. Or where she had been then. She could only remember the room with the white bed and the fig tree outside the window. And she remembered when some of the other children came for her. One of Tete's boys. No, maybe it was these. And they said, *It's Christmas, Aunt Ode.* And they took her home with them and gave her a box of dusting powder and when she was leaving she started to cry and the girl said, *Now, Aunt Ode, if you're going to cry, you're going to spoil our Christmas.* So she quit crying. And the boy said, *We want you to be happy, Aunt Ode. We like to bring you home with us, but we want you to be happy.*

The boy stopped the car. He said, "Aunt Ode, you remember this house, don't you?" She looked out of the window. It was a big frame house. It had a wide front porch and steps with banisters. There was a swing on the porch and there was a nigra woman in the swing. "No," she said.

"Yes, you do, Aunt Ode," the boy said. She took a good

look. She saw two nigra children in the yard. One of them sailed the top of a lard can and it landed on the roof. "Just a nigra house," she said.

"That used to be your house, Aunt Ode," the boy said. I must have forgotten, she thought. "When I was a boy," he said, "I used to come and visit you. There was a catalpa tree in the yard then." Yes, she thought, there was a catalpa tree in the front yard. "And you used to keep ferns on the porch." Ferns on the porch, she thought. And on the back porch there was latticework. And suddenly it came to her. This was the house, this was the place she had tried to remember. There was a hall. There was a room at the end of the hall. Bob had died there, one night he waked up sick, and behind those windows on the far side of the porch was the parlor where they had laid the body out. There were so many flowers. She could smell them still. "Bob died the ninth of July," she said. And the boy said, "I remember Uncle Bob."

"It was a Friday," she said.

"He was tall," the boy said, "and I never saw him without his hat on."

"Yes," she said, "he was tall." She looked at the house again, and she remembered coming here before. To collect the rent. Only the people on the porch were white. There were white children in the yard, and one of them said, *Who are you, lady?* And she said, *I used to live here.* And he asked her when. *Oh, a long time ago,* she said. I wonder when it was? she thought.

The boy opened the door. "You sit here, Aunt Ode," he said. "I'm going to collect the rent." But she said, "You children . . ."

"Don't forget," the girl said. "They're behind five dollars."

"You children don't know," she said. The boy had come around the car. He stopped and looked at her. "I want to get out," she said. And the girl said, "Aunt Ode, you better stay here."

"I want to get out," she said. She tried to open the door. The boy said, "Aunt Ode, you want to go with me to get the rent?" And she nodded. And the girl said, "Bubba . . ." And he said, "It's all right, Polly." And she said, "Well, I won't be responsible."

He opened the door and reached in after her. Miss Odell stepped out. The ground felt funny under her. The boy had her arm and he was walking her up the walk and the nigra children were watching her. The woman in the swing had gone inside. "Now you be careful going up these steps, Aunt Ode," the boy said. "You know you're not sixteen." And he laughed, and she laughed, and she thought, I was twenty when he brought me here. She felt the steps under her and she felt the boy's arm on hers, and above her and ahead of her she saw the screen door and the nigra woman standing behind it. "How you doing, Aunt Ode?" the boy said, and she said, "I'm doing just fine," and she felt him holding her.

The nigra woman said, "Good evening," and the boy said, "Good evening," and they walked up on the porch. "We came to collect the rent," he said.

"I won't have it before Saturday," the nigra woman said.

"It was due the twentieth," he said.

"Well, I'll see . . ." the woman said. She left the door for a minute and came back unrolling something in her hand. "Here's fifteen dollars," she said. "I can let you have the rest the first of the month."

She opened the screen and Miss Odell could see inside. She could see the hall and she remembered that there had been a hatrack in the hall and a bookcase, and all those books, her papa's books. He had written his name in them, and dates, and things like *Rained today—won't get hands into fields.* And sometimes sad things, there in an Appleton's Encyclopedia, at the top of some page where he thought no one would find it: *My precious Vashti died today.*

The nigra woman was holding the door open. Miss Odell took a step. She took another step and she could smell the hall and she knew she was inside. The boy still had her by the arm. "We got to go, Aunt Ode," he said.

"Just in a minute," she said.

The boy said, "Miss Odell used to live here," and the nigra woman said, "Yes, sir."

"You children don't know what it's like," she said, and it all came back to her, those years, the people, all of it. "The parlor's in here," she said, and she took another step and he was holding her, and then she took another and he went along with her. She saw the fireplace and the windows that opened on the porch and she could smell the flowers in the room. "There were so many flowers," she said. The boy said, "Aunt Ode, we got to be getting back. We don't want to tire you." I'm already tired, she thought. I been tired so long now. And she wanted to sleep, and dream, past any awakening.

She sank into a chair. "Aunt Ode . . ." the boy said. She closed her eyes. There *was* a place, she thought. "This isn't your house . . ."

"That's all right," the nigra woman said. "She can sit there."

"Aunt Ode . . ."

"In a minute," she said.

"Now, Aunt Ode," he said, "if you don't come on, we're not going to want to take you for a drive again."

I don't care, Miss Odell thought.

He tried to take her by the arm. Outside a car horn blew. "Polly's blowing for us . . ." he said.

I'm here, she thought. In a minute he'll take me away and he'll never bring me back again. None of the children will. They won't come on Sundays to take me for drives and they won't give me dusting powder for Christmas . . .

"Aunt Ode . . ."

But I don't care, she thought.

Where the Music Was

I wasn't the only one. The others used to stand there, too, watching the freights go by; and we used to climb the water tank, because somebody, maybe it was Bubba Tims, said you could see Memphis if you tried. You couldn't, of course. You could barely see the Bogue. Not even that: the gin this side of it. But we looked. And we talked about what we were going to do. Bubba was going to be a pilot in the Army Air Force. He's crop-dusting now. J.C. was going to play in Jimmy Dorsey's band. And he was good, but I guess not good enough. He had a band of his own for a while; played for all of the Legion Club dances. I was going to run me a service station. They put that in the class prophecy: *We look*

*in the crystal ball and we see Ben Hadley checking the oil in
Bitsy Conner's Oldsmobile.* . . . The closest I came to running a service station was wiping windshields at the Red
Front Billups on Saturdays. That's the way it is. You're always going to do something. You never do. Maybe it's a
good thing you don't know that in the beginning; I guess if
you did you'd go out and shoot yourself, or maybe do like
Bubba did: write SHIT across the water tank. You can imagine how that went over. They hauled us all in, and our folks
gave us a licking, and Bubba's old man had to pay to have
that word removed. Only they didn't do such a good job. I
guess if you look good now you can still see it.

I don't know what it was, why we had to get away from
here. Maybe people everywhere, wherever they are, have to
get away from there. But I think we had to most of all. It
was worse at night. Then you could smell the air from the
river, the tar and the towboats, and you could hear the
swing chains on all those porches. Every house had a porch
and every porch had a swing, and that sound was like a
clock. The talk you heard on those porches was complaining: the rain was bad for the crops and the highway was
coming through the wrong side of town and Roosevelt was
going to get us in the war and the nigras were uppity. Some
nights we used to go and shoot the street lights out. "Man,"
Bubba said, "I got to get away from here."

That summer he hitchhiked a ride to Chicago, and later he
told us it was a fairy who picked him up and the fairy paid
for everything. That was the summer we graduated, and I
guess I would have left here then but I got me a job on the
highway, clearing right of way. The next summer I got laid
off (they caught me sleeping on the job) and I had saved a
little money and I figured it was time. Besides, I was mixed
up with this girl. She was married to one of the fellows on
the road gang, only he couldn't do her any good. That's what

she said. Well, I was doing her pretty good, but you got to watch your step. So I hauled on out of here, bought me a bus ticket to Memphis and rode the train from there.

I always wanted to see Chicago, even before Bubba went. The truth is, I used to listen to the radio late at night, after I had gone to bed, and the music they played came from the Aragon Ballroom. *This music is coming to you from the Aragon Ballroom,* they used to say, *just a few minutes from the heart of downtown Chicago.* And I used to imagine I was there. Not dancing. I never could dance. Just there where the music was. And it was cold there; there was snow on the streets. That was the way I thought of it. When I think of Chicago now I think of how it was that night: the wind warm and the sky red and the noise the El makes when it turns into Wabash. Only later you never notice it. It was close to midnight when the train got in, and I spent half the night just walking, just looking, because this was what I had thought about, up there on the water tank. And when I found me a room and hit the bed I couldn't even sleep. I just laid there. "Man," I said, "this is it." I thought it was. It was like the first time. But it never is the same again. Those streets never looked so long again; those buildings never looked so tall.

It didn't matter. I was there. I was ready to stay, all right. The first week I got me a job working the counter in a hash house off LaSalle. This Greek ran it, and I saw his sign in the window and he hired me on the spot. Two to ten, six days a week. When I used to do things was at night. I'd get off from work at ten o'clock and I'd go and have a beer, or maybe shoot some pool, or see a picture show. Sometimes I'd ride the El. I'd catch the El on Lake Street and I'd ride it on out, looking down on all those streets and houses and wondering: who lives in those houses? A lot of people, and you'll never get to know a one of them. Did you ever think that? Pass some people on a street and wonder who they were, and know you'd never know, and think: somebody does. When you get right down to it, we know almost nobody, almost nobody knows us, and I used to think that on the El, looking down on those houses. That was why I couldn't stay, I guess. After a while I got to wondering. Nobody ever looked at me. Nobody said, "Ben Hadley." Nobody said, "Ben Hadley, what you doing here?" I guess if they had I'd have said, "Having a time, man." That's the way you do.

I said you never get to know a one of them. You don't. Not the Greek. He kept to himself, talked to himself, never said much to me. But there were three I almost got to know, and didn't, which is like saying you almost ran a service station, or almost took a girl to bed with you—almost doesn't count for much. One of them was Tip. Which was funny. Tip was a nigra. I guess he was the only nigra I ever almost knew. The others were just nigras—yardmen and nurses and cooks. They were there all your life but you never looked at them; or if you did, you thought: they're all alike, they look alike, and their houses smell alike. Did you ever go in a nigra house? They have a funny smell, like coal oil and scorched shirts. I never went in Tip's house, so I never knew the smell of it. I only saw Tip at work. He worked in the kitchen, he was a dishwasher, and he had been to night school a year. Oh, he was smart. "You want me to name all the Vice-Presidents?" he would say. And he could name all the Vice-Presidents. But sometimes he'd stop and laugh. "What's the percentage?" he'd say.

The funny part was, Tip came from this part of the country, too. He was born over in Sunflower County, and he knew I knew what it was like, but we never said anything. It was the same as if we had known the same people, gone to school in the same school, but I could never talk to him

27

without thinking of what it was like: standing at those back doors. That wasn't what Tip remembered, though. What he remembered was cotton and china trees and the smell of dust before a rain and the way the sun comes up. Only once he was talking about his brother Richard. He said his brother Richard went back down South and opened up a pressing shop. And then he said, because he wanted me to understand, a *colored* pressing shop. And I smiled. And he smiled, too. And he said, "I'd like to go back there myself. You know, just to see where I was born." I didn't ask him why. I mean, why he'd want to go back, even to see where he was born. But I guess I thought of it.

That night we rode the El I forgot for a minute who Tip was. Maybe for a minute he forgot who I was. We were riding the El, it was after we got off from work, and he said, "You doing anything?" And I said, "No." And he said, "Why don't you come by my place? My sister'll fix us something." He lived with his sister. And I said, "Okay." It was late and I was tired, I guess. And then I remembered and I said, "I guess some other time." Tip didn't say anything. I guess he knew then who I was and who he was, and maybe he wondered who that white man was, who put that blood in him. "Well, here's where I get off," he said. "See you tomorrow." And I said, "Yeah." And he got off. He was standing there on the platform, just a light-skin nigra boy, and maybe he knew what I was thinking: that I was sorry. But that's not enough, is it?

I never told Mr. Flynn about Tip. I never would have told Mr. Flynn anything. I tell you who he reminded me of. There was an old man named Caraway. I guess he wasn't even old, but we thought he was. He used to get the boys behind the schoolhouse, and you know the kind of things he'd say. What you could do to make it grow. Things like that. And he had this laugh. Mr. Flynn had it, too. I don't

mean he said the same kind of things. He didn't. But it gave
you the creeps to have him close to you. His room was near
the stairs. I think he used to listen at his door, and when I'd
come up the steps he'd be there looking down at me. "Hey,
boy," he'd say, and when he talked to you he'd get so close
you could smell the Vicks-salve on his breath. "I got something you might like to see." He showed me twice. A picture
he had. It was faded brown, and torn, but you could make
out what it was: a nigra bound with rope, lying in the back
of a wagon. "That's Charley Hubbard," Mr. Flynn would
say. "You heard of Charley Hubbard, didn't you?" He was
there when they burned Charley Hubbard, and he said
Charley Hubbard cussed a white man when they put the
torch to him. "You know what he done?" Mr. Flynn said. I
never heard of Charley Hubbard. "Had his way with this
white girl." Mr. Flynn smiled. "That's why I come north," he
said. "To get away from the nigras. Now they're coming
north, too. It won't be long, the nigras'll be taking over Chicago."

I guess Mr. Flynn would have said a lot of things if I had
given him a chance to talk. But I was always going in or out,
trying to miss him when I could. "I like you, boy," he'd say.
"You know why? I come from the South myself. I was born
and raised in the South. Me and you, we know what it is."

One night that summer when I went back to the boarding
house Mr. Flynn wasn't there. His daughter had come for
him, to put him in an old folks' home. I never knew he had a
daughter; he never mentioned her. But he left an envelope.
He had printed my name on the outside in brown ink. On
the inside was that picture. Charley Hubbard. And on the
back of it he wrote KEEP THIS TO REMIND YOU. For a long
time I kept it, just to remind me.

The other was Ollie. She looked like her name: big eyes,
straggly yellow hair, a face that was closer to pretty than

ugly, and when she smiled you forgot her hair, her eyes, everything; she was Ollie. I used to see her in this bar, maybe a half a dozen times before I ever said a word to her. She was that way. You wanted to say something but you knew you better not. Only one night we got to talking. I had had enough, I was ready to go home, and I guess I must have told her that.

"Where's home?" she said.

"Mississippi," I said.

"I used to have a girl friend," she said. "She came from Mississippi."

"Maybe I know her," I said.

"No," she said. "You don't know her. Her daddy put her away. She wasn't even crazy, but she was going to marry this boy and her daddy put her away."

That was how we got to talking. You know how one thing leads to another. And then I asked her where she was from, and she said no place.

"You're not from here," I said.

"Nobody's from here," she said, and she kind of smiled. There was a mirror in front of her. "I'm from Talladega, Alabama. I'm twenty-four and I been married twice and I'm not going to make the same mistake again."

"What you doing here?" I said.

For a minute she didn't say anything. She kept looking into that mirror, like she saw something I didn't or couldn't. "You want to go where we can talk?" she said.

So we went up to her room to talk. And that was all we did, which was not the way I figured it. I figured her to be like all the rest of them. Maybe it's not what they really want, but they know it's what you want. "It's not you," she said. "And it's not that I don't want to. I mean, sometimes I want to."

"You never told me your name," I said.

"Ollie," she said.

And I told her I was Ben.

"You don't look like Ben," she said. "I knew a boy once . . ." She laughed. "You look like Barn." After that she called me Barn.

"What's it like?" she said.

"What?" I said.

"The place you come from."

"Oh, it's not much town," I said. "Half of it sits on one side of the Y & MV railroad tracks and the other half sits on the other, and when you climb the water tank you can almost see the Bogue."

"What's the Bogue?" she said.

"That's a river," I said. And I told her it was green with willows, and sometimes we got drunk by moonlight and swam in it. "Moody Bailey drowned."

"Did you ever wonder how it would be to drown?" she said.

"No," I said.

"It might be nice," she said, and her eyes were as green as willows by the Bogue. "I mean, it might not take long."

"You're crazy," I said.

"I know," she said. All the time we talked the radio was on. Not loud but low. And when I leaned across the bed to turn it off, she said, "Don't."

I looked at her.

"It's not the same," she said.

"Without the music?"

"At night," she said. "Don't you hate for dark to come?"

I guess I must have laughed at that.

"I mean it," she said. And then she said, "You're not going to leave, are you?"

"No," I said, "I'm not going to leave."

So I stayed with her that night. The next night too. And

all we did that night was talk. Some nights we did more than talk. Maybe because it was what I wanted and she had her music anyway. I guess I'd be there yet. But I had had enough, I was ready to go home, and she was what decided me.

"You got to go back too," I said.

"I can't," she said.

"You got to go back to Talladega, Alabama."

"You know what it's like?" she said. I guess I had wondered that. "I live in a two-story house and I got a Packard car and charge accounts in Birmingham and my daddy treats me just like he did my mama. I guess he'd give me the moon if I wanted it, only . . ."

"Only what?" I said.

She laughed. "Only it's not the moon I want," she said.

"What is it?"

"No," she said. "You won't find it. If you tell, you won't find it."

"Is it here?" I said.

She looked at me. I knew what she was thinking: it might be.

I hope it was, and that she found it. Maybe not in Chicago but somewhere. I thought that whatever it was she was looking for I could give her, but I was nineteen then, and that wasn't what she meant. Maybe she was looking for what we all were looking for, back there on the water tank. A place. Maybe a place where the dark never comes. Or, for Tip, where the houses have no back doors. Or, for me, where the music was. I went to the Aragon Ballroom that summer. I rode out on the bus and I walked through those doors and into that lobby and out onto that dance floor with the artificial sky. Oh, it was big. I guess half of Chicago was out on the dance floor. And then a little before eleven the band stopped playing and the couples stopped dancing and a man came out on the stage and held up his hand, and when he gave the signal the band started to play again and you could hear him say, "This music is coming to you from the Aragon Ballroom . . ." It gave you a funny feeling, knowing you were there, right there where the music was. But it wasn't the same. I mean, those nights in bed, the way I had imagined it.

So I rode the train back home. I worked at the Red Front on Saturdays, and when I got this offer to work for the telephone company I took them up on it. I married one of the Clanton girls from across the Bogue, and we got a boy who's as bad as Bubba ever was. Times don't change, do they? Except in funny ways. I never listen to the radio any more. And I never climb anything higher than a telephone pole. You can't see Memphis from there. But sometimes I get the crazy idea I'd like to go to Chicago again. And I think of Tip and Mr. Flynn and Ollie, three people I almost knew, but didn't, three people who almost knew me, but didn't. And then I think: maybe it's a good thing.

Stopover

Two figures broke the rectangle of dark between cars. Across the coupling, face to face, they stood, their legs apart; danced like spring-wound toys to the roll and pitch of the train. The dance was out of time, the movement of a thousand miles of rail, a thousand no-name towns, days, nights, faces, all left behind and lost. The whistle blew, the brakes went on for the crossing: Mississippi Law Stop. The cars rumbled past the crossing, past the auto idling there, its headlights picking out for a moment the two figures—one a boy and the other an old man.

They had ridden the rails together south and east, north and west, from Carbondale, Illinois, to here (and that was a long time ago). Gar was the boy, and he talked; and Lou listened, with the indifference of a man who had done a lot of listening. He had done a lot of traveling, too, and he knew the roads and some of the timetables and which towns to get off in and which to stay on in.

Gar sometimes still remembered the way his mother looked, the way his old man fell across the bed drunk when she died, and sometimes he wondered what became of his sister Callie. Callie was pretty; she always saw the funny side. He wondered if she had married and if she had pretty kids, and if she had forgiven him for the things he said when he went away.

Lou did not wonder anything, and if he remembered anything it was something in the far distance, before Carbondale or Cairo. He had the patient air of a man waiting, a man who had perhaps left the depot waiting room and climbed upon the train to finish out his wait.

They were here together, tonight, riding the rails north, because Gar was waiting, too. The whistle blew. The freight began to slacken speed. "She's stopping," Lou said.

Gar leaned to one side. Ahead, the lights of a town burned cold, shimmering like winter stars. "Coming into a town. Reckon we better jump for it?"

"I got a hunch," Lou said.

"What's your hunch?"

"I got a hunch we better."

Gar drew back in. "What say we ride her through? They not going to be checking this time of night."

"Listen what I tell you," Lou said. "I was raised in one of these slow-freight towns. You want to chop some cotton?"

Gar laughed. "What's chances for? They never caught us yet, did they?"

The cars jerked, jerked again, jolted to a stop. There was no sound except the flap-flap-flap of truck tires along the road paralleling the rails. The truck roared past, taillights marking its path into the distance. A slow shudder ran the length of the freight.

"What was the last town?"

"Christ," Gar said, "we been through a lot of towns. One looks like the next to me."

"Maybe Boyle."

"You know these towns, don't you?"

"I ought to," Lou said.

For a minute they stood there, listening. Then Gar let go of his hold, swung down on the coupling. "Say, Lou . . ."

"Yeah?"

"That town you was from . . ." He was thinking of Callie. "Where was that?"

Lou reached in his pocket. "Texas."

"You ever wanted to go back there?"

He took out a harp.

"I mean, didn't you ever . . ." Gar stopped. He lowered his voice. "There's somebody out there," he said.

They both listened.

"Want me to take a look and see?"

Lou nodded.

Gar leaned to one side. Up the tracks he saw the headlights of a car. Between him and the lights he saw the figure of a man.

"You see anything?"

Gar pulled back in. He nodded. "Right on us. Want to run for it?"

"Too late," Lou said. "Flatten up against the car. Don't move."

They stepped back against the cars. As they did, a light was turned upon them. A voice from behind the light said, "Jump down, boys. This here's the end of the line."

"Do what he tells you," Lou said.

"I got a forty-five on you," the man said, "so don't try nothing funny."

Lou slipped the harp back in his pocket and climbed down, the boy by the side of him.

"You want the cuffs on or you want it the easy way?"

"We just want a break," Lou said. "Give us a break and that's the last you seen of us."

"I heard that before." The man laughed. "Truth is, we need you boys. We got a lot of cotton needs chopping. Start walking up that way."

"Look, sheriff," Lou said, "the boy here's sick. Honest to God. He's been heaving blood since Corpus and we was headed for the vet's hospital."

"I ain't the sheriff." The man turned the light in Gar's face. "And this here boy don't look old enough to be a vet nohow. What was you in, son?"

"The Merchant Marine," Gar said.

"Hunh. No wonder we near about lost the war. You boys get going up that way."

They walked up alongside the freight to a cinder patch where an old sedan was parked. "Get in the back," the man said. They climbed in the back seat next to a bird dog scratching fleas with her hind leg. "That's Lady," the man said. "Get over there, Lady."

A man came up on the other side of the car, waving a light. "Any luck?" he said.

"I picked up a couple. How about you?"

"Hell, I had me a nigra but he broke and run." He flashed his light in the back seat. "Say, you got a real old-timer here. How long you been riding the rails, old man?"

"The boy here's sick. We was headed for the vet's hospital," Lou said.

"Think you up a new one, old man. You got that train-smoke smell. How many jails you been in?"

"Give us a break, mister."

"What about you, boy? How many jails you wrote your name in?"

Gar looked at the man.

"I'm talking to you, boy."

"And I'm listening," Gar said.

"Kind of smarty, ain't you?"

"The boy don't mean nothing," Lou said.

"We don't like smarties. Maybe we was going to let you go if you hadn't gone and got smarty."

"Turn us loose and you won't see no more of us," Lou said.

"What about you, smarty? Let's hear you do a little begging."

"I ain't begging you for nothing," Gar said.

"Okay by me," the man said. "Start her up, Clovis." He hoisted himself into the front seat.

The sedan started down the cinder drive, turned left onto the main road and into the corporate limits of town, half-circled a Confederate monument that stood in the center of the street, ringed with freshly whitewashed chains. An oncoming car swung the other arc of the circle, backfiring. At the far end of the street, the sedan turned into the courthouse grounds; its headlights swept the width of the building and came to rest upon the jail.

"I guess you know what that is, don't you?" said one of the men. He laughed. "It may not be the fanciest jail you was ever in . . ."

"But they won't be seeing much of it nohow," the other said. "Reckon they'll like the farm?"

"Oh, I reckon they'll learn to."

The men got out of the car. One opened the back door. "Okay, pile out," he said.

"Watch and see Lady don't get out," the other man said. He shined his light on the jail. "That way. In and up. We'll book you in the morning."

The cell they took them to was full, so a trusty brought in mattresses. The men in the bunks were asleep. They came awake suddenly, cursing and shielding their eyes from the light; as suddenly, they lay still and watched. One wore army shorts. The other wore nothing to hide his nakedness. Their bodies were white; their faces were red, from the same sun, and they had the spider-cautious look of hard-year sharecroppers.

"Look here, Albert. Look here at the pokey bait," the one in shorts said, drawling.

"Yeah. And we been wishing we had a little company. Wonder what they in for?"

"What you boys in for?"

Gar dropped down on a mattress. "Riding the rails."

"Riding the rails?"

"They picked us off the freight," he said.

"This time of night? Man, they sure must be short of hands at the farm."

"Parchman?" Lou said.

"Naw," the one in shorts said. "Not the state pen. The county farm."

The one called Albert laughed. "You're lucky," he said.

Gar looked at him. "How you mean?"

"I mean you're lucky. They hold you here three . . . four days. Time for your prints to clear. Then you chop for thirty days and you're on your way. Now us . . ."

"Yeah," the other said. "They got different plans for us."

"What you up for?" Gar said.

Albert laughed. "You want to tell him, Price?"

The one in shorts was Price. He was booked for attempted

murder and his trial was coming up. He had got word his girl was shacking up with a truck driver out of Memphis, so he waylaid the bastard, whipped him bad.

"Left him for dead," Albert said. "Hell, it was him or Price, and Price gets in there first."

"What about you?" Gar said.

"Me?" Albert grinned.

"Moonshining," Price said. "They caught him running it over from the Arkansas side. Caught his brother, too, but he got away."

"It wasn't only moonshine," Albert said. "My brother and me, we had killed some deer out of season. They was after us for that. This nigra told them where we'd be, the bastard. My brother, he broke and run. Got clean away. They figure I know where he's at. Maybe I do. But you know something?" He grinned. "I ain't going to tell."

Albert, true to his word, did not tell. But there were other stories to tell, and he told them, and Price had his own stories to tell, and he told them. Their stories were about the women they had and how they had them, about coon hunts, manhunts, stories of quicksand deaths, seed-house births, planting time, plowing time, lean years, fat years, floods, droughts, and the long arm of God Almighty. Through two days they told their stories, some of them twice, but when lights-out came they slept. Then Lou and Gar, lying face up in the darkness, talked.

"Say, Lou," Gar said.

Lou said, "Yeah?"

"What you thinking about?"

"Oh," Lou said, "the jails I been in."

Gar laughed. "They all smell alike. You ever notice that?"

Lou said, "Yeah."

"The first time I was ever in jail . . . I guess I must've been thirteen or fourteen. We broke some street lights. Jack

Owen and B.C. and Brother and me. Anyhow," he said, "they locked us up overnight. I guess I was pretty scared. Not so much about being in jail as what my old man would say. You know what he said?" Gar laughed. " 'They should've kept you,' he said."

"He's dead, ain't he?" Lou said.

"Yeah," Gar said. "He's dead."

For a long time they lay still. Off in the distance a whistle blew, a dog barked. "You hear that?" Gar said.

Lou said, "Yeah." He sat up and took out his harp, began to play, low, each note held like a long breath.

"You got something on your mind," Gar said. "What is it?"

Lou took the harp away from his mouth for a moment. "Nothing," he said. He went on playing.

"If it hadn't been for me, they'd have let us go. I should've kept my mouth shut. That's what you're thinking, ain't it?"

Lou put the harp away. "You got a lot to learn, boy."

"Like what?"

Lou laughed. "Like a lot of things, I guess."

"Say what you're trying to say."

"That's it."

"You got a lot to learn yourself," Gar said. "You rode so many rails you don't know nothing else. What's it gotten you?"

"That's what I mean." Lou laughed again. "I been around. You—you got a lot to see, places to go . . ."

"You're saying this here's where you get off. That what's you're saying, ain't it?"

"For Christ's sake, pipe down so we can get some sleep," Price said.

"Okay, okay," Gar said. He lowered his voice. "If that's how you want it, okay by me."

Lou slapped a mosquito, rubbed his hand across his knee. "You got it all figured, don't you?" he said.

"Yeah, I got it figured."

"All wrong," Lou said.

"For Christ's sake, shut up!" Price yelled. "Before I come over there and shut you up!"

"So you can get some sleep?" Gar said.

"So we can all get some fuckin' sleep," Albert said.

"Getting up early or something?"

"Yeah," Albert said. "I got a early morning train to catch."

When daylight came, they awoke and they talked, and their stories were the same. The sun rose in the sky, sweeping the wall and then the floor, and the air in the cell grew hot. "I had a girl one time," Albert said, "named Eva, and I guess I would've married her, but you know how it is."

"What become of her?" Price said.

"Oh, she run off with a Kroger butcher," Albert said. "Not long after that, she got hit by a taxicab on the main street of Jackson and killed right out. Which just goes to show . . ."

Price said, "What?"

Albert grinned. "Don't fool around with no Kroger butcher," he said.

The sun climbed higher, and they talked, and their stories were the same. Noon came, and afternoon. Then the cell door swung open and they looked up and saw the sheriff standing there, and he said, "Howdy, boys," and they said, "Howdy."

"You boys ever hear of somebody named Denham?"

None of them said anything.

"You right sure?"

Price said, "There used to be some Denhams over on the Bogue."

"Not this one," the sheriff said. He looked at Lou. "You know this one, don't you, old man?"

Lou nodded.

The sheriff pulled a piece of paper out of his pocket, unfolded it and began to read. "Louis Ted Denham, alias Lou T. Denham, alias Lou T. Dunham, five-foot eight, one thirty-five, brown hair . . ." He looked up, smiled. "Kind of gray now. Been a long time, ain't it, Denham?"

"I guess maybe it was," Lou said.

"Where you been since you skipped Parchman in 'thirty-four?" The sheriff looked at the piece of paper again. "Sent up from Sunflower County. Served a little better than three years." He folded the paper and put it back in his pocket. "They had just about give you up," he said.

"Sent up for what?" Gar said.

"I'll let Denham here tell you," the sheriff said. He looked at Lou. "We're going to be taking you back tomorrow. About noon. How's it feel to be going back?"

Lou smiled.

"You should've stayed away, Denham." The sheriff stood there for a moment, as if there was something more he wanted to say. Then he turned and walked out of the cell.

Lou got up, Price and Albert watching him. He walked to the window.

"What they trying to do?" Gar said. "They trying to hang something on you you didn't do?"

Lou shook his head.

"Sent up for what?"

"Manslaughter," he said.

Price smiled. "Damned if you didn't have us fooled," he said. "Damned if you didn't have me and Albert fooled."

"Yeah," Albert said. "Manslaughter."

"Why didn't you tell me?" Gar said.

Lou turned and looked at him. He turned back to the window, cupped his hands over his mouth, and called to someone on the gravel below. "Hey, sheriff. I got something to ask you."

"Yeah?" came the voice from below. "What you want, Denham?"

"The boy. The boy here with me. He never got in no trouble. How about letting him go, sheriff?"

"That's kind of a big order, ain't it, Denham?"

"Not for you, sheriff. All you got to do is say so. I'm going back and I'm asking you as a favor."

"Okay, Denham. I'll think about it." Footsteps moved away on the gravel.

Lou left the window, stretched out on a mattress, his hands under his head. Gar went and sat next to him. "What you going to do?" he said.

"Nothing."

"We could try to make a break for it."

Lou shook his head.

"Not even try?"

"It was bound to happen, sooner or later."

"Why was it you never told me?" Gar said.

Lou rolled over on his stomach. "You never did ask me. Anyway," he said, "it was a long time ago."

Toward late afternoon they came to let Gar go, to send him on his way, like Lou wanted, like the sheriff said. "Luck to you, boy," Lou said. "Let me hear from you sometime."

"Yeah," Gar said.

"What you going to do?"

"I don't know." Gar smiled. "Maybe stop off some place. What's a good place?"

"I never found any," Lou said. "That's the trouble. I kept looking, but I never found any."

Gar went out between them, down the iron steps to the outside. When he looked up from the gravel walk, he saw

Lou standing at the window, saw him wave, a quick motion of his hand across his face. Then he walked away, past the crape myrtle bushes and the row of parked cars toward the Confederate monument down the street.

He kept walking. He walked up one side of the street and down the other, and dark came and he sat on a bench in front of a café, thinking what he'd eat if he had the money to eat with. A fan blew greasy smells out onto the street, and the waitress through the glass window looked like Callie, like Callie used to look. A man picking his teeth with a toothpick came out and propped one foot on the bench and said, "Hot."

"Say, mister," Gar said, "how's about staking me to a cup of coffee?"

"Hunh," the man said, and handed him a dime.

Gar sat at the counter inside and drank his coffee, but inside the waitress did not look much like Callie and the coffee only warmed his hunger. He went back outside and walked some more.

He spent the night in an abandoned shed beside the tracks, propped against a post, awake, remembering his mother's face, Callie's face, the no-name towns. At last, toward daybreak, he fell asleep. When he opened his eyes again, the sun was up and the air was blue with summer smoke. A towheaded boy ran around and around the shed looking in.

Gar called to him.

The boy aimed his toy pistol and said bang-bang, running.

"When's the next freight go through?"

The boy's circles narrowed and soon he stopped, just beyond reach. "What you want?" he said.

"Tell me when the next freight's through and I might give you something. You want something?"

"What?" the boy said. "Let me see what you got."

Gar dug one hand into his pants pocket and drew it out. "Here," he said. "You can have it."

The boy stared at the dark object. "What is it?"

"A buckeye. You never seen a buckeye?"

"What's it do?"

"Brings you luck. Anything you want, maybe."

The boy dropped the toy pistol and shifted the buckeye from one hand to the other, turned it over so that it shone dully in the morning sun. Then he locked it in his fist and ran, out over the tracks a way, looked back and kept running.

Gar walked back into the shed and sat where the shade was cool and the ground cool and the mold on the bricks smelled clean. He sat a long time and after a while he heard the whistle and the chuff-chuff-chuff and he got up and went outside and saw the freight coming through slow, the way he and Lou had come. He stood there by the tracks, so close that the engine blew steam over him and the ground shook; he could reach out with his hand, swing up if he wanted to, but the freight went by, the caboose went by, and he straddled the track to watch it go.

When it had disappeared from sight, the smoke blown past, he walked over to where the toy pistol had fallen, picked it up, held it in his hand. All at once he slipped it into his pocket and started walking fast, around the shed to the street and down the street toward the courthouse grounds. He walked without looking back, and he went and stood in the crape myrtle bushes, looking up at the jail. Later he squatted; much later he sat; then he stood again, waiting, and the sun climbed higher in the sky. Once he heard the sound of laughter. Once he heard the notes of a harp, played softly, held like a long breath.

So he waited, and the sun climbed straight up overhead,

and he saw the men come, and he knew what they had come for. So he waited, and then stood, one hand stuck in his pocket hard. He saw them come into the outside, out of the jail, and he saw Lou between them. He saw them come down the gravel walk by the crape myrtle bushes to the row of cars. Lou was saying something and one of the men was saying something, and he heard them without hearing what they said. They came close and his hand swung out, the toy pistol in it, black and ugly in the light, and he hollered, "Run for it, Lou! I got you covered! Run!"

The two men stopped still, like play statues, and Lou stopped still, and the sun was overhead. Then the play statues came alive: one plunged into the crape myrtle bushes; the other stepped behind Lou, pinning his arms together at the back. A shot was fired, and another. The man who had plunged into the crape myrtle bushes stumbled out, breathing hard. The pistol in his hand glittered in the light. "Sonofabitch," he said. "Sonofabitch." People came running. They ran from all directions and they stopped short of the crape myrtle bushes and they asked who it was that was shot.

The man with the pistol told everybody to get back there, and the other man handcuffed Lou and shoved him through the crowd to the row of cars. "Who was he?" the man said.

Lou shook his head.

"You heard me," the man said.

"You wouldn't know if I told you," Lou said.

"I see him," cried a voice from out of the crowd. "See. See, back up under there."

The
Ears of
the
World

Some people are born to do one thing, and some another, and I guess Miss Willie was one of those people born to write. She used to say that herself—oh, a long while ago—only nobody paid much attention at the time. They let it go in one ear and out the other, and they kept right on talking themselves. And Miss Willie kept on listening. Which was how they wanted it: everybody loves to talk, and nobody much likes to listen. "The world is all mouth and no ears," Miss Willie used to say. So she was going to be the ears of the world. And for a good while she was. Everybody called Miss Willie, because they knew she would listen and because they wanted to talk.

When it first started, they didn't have much to talk about.
They did, but they didn't want to talk about *that*. So the
talking they did at first was about trifling things—who was
born and who had died, and who was going to die (cancer
or otherwise), everything, in fact, but what they really
wanted to talk about. The more talking they did, the more
they found to say. Talking is like that, like anything else—
it's habit-forming, so to speak. And it got so they couldn't
talk unless Miss Willie would listen; a good deal of her time
was just taken up listening. After a while, she let her house
go. Her yard too. The grass grew and she didn't seem to
notice, or, if she did, to care. When she was younger, she
was right particular. Everything had to be *just so*. If she
went to the store to buy a piece of goods, she had to wear a
hat. All that changed. It got so she was always on the go,
and too busy going to stop and fix herself. She kept a hair
net on her hair and her stockings rolled, and the dress she
wore was likely as not the one she wore the day before. "I
know I look a sight," she'd say. But nobody cared. What
they cared about was that Miss Willie was there to listen.

"Willie, honey," Lucy Pembleton would say, "are you doing anything?"

And Miss Willie would say no, she wasn't doing anything.

"Well, come right over," Lucy Pembleton would say. "I
got something I want to talk to you about."

Maybe Lucy had done it again: fallen head over heels for
some younger man who didn't have a dime—or a pot to pee
in, as Lucy had a way of putting it. Oh, she knew her faults.
One time it was a bus driver out of Memphis. Lucy rode
down on the 10:05 with him, and after that she was off to
Memphis every chance she got. Another time it was a CCC
boy, maybe nineteen, and she was close to thirty then. They
wound up in the Chisca Hotel and they wrote their names in

a Gideon Bible, and that was the closest she ever came to marrying.

"You want to know why? I'll tell you why," Lucy Pembleton would say. And Miss Willie would listen.

While she was listening, she might get another call. People called around. If they didn't find her one place, they called another; there were not that many places anyway. So if Nola Day didn't catch Miss Willie at home, which, as a general rule, she didn't, she'd call her to the phone at Lucy Pembleton's. Or at Ouida Woods', or Gladys Wilkinson's—wherever it was she happened to be.

"Hello, Willie," she'd say. "Nola. How you feeling?"

"Pretty well," Miss Willie would say, which might mean anything. She was never the complaining kind.

"That's good. This heat . . . I bet you it's a hundred in the shade. Listen, Willie," she'd say, "I got to talk to you."

"Well, I'm at Lucy's . . ."

"I declare, I had a time reaching you. You going to be there long?"

"Well, I'll see," Miss Willie might say. Or, "Not long." It all depended on what it was that Lucy had to talk about.

"I got to talk to you," Nola would say. "I can't tell you on the phone. Can you drop by here on your way home?"

Maybe it was noon when Miss Willie dropped by. She was always on the go at noon, taking pot luck, which in Nola's case was a half a head of lettuce with Thousand Island dressing. Or a bowl of cream of chicken soup. Canned soup. I don't guess Nola ever made a pot of soup in her life, unless it was before she married Bennie Day. She married Bennie and he died and left her well provided for: that house with twenty rooms and a sleeping porch (and no one there but Nola half the time) and all that money. Lord knows how much money. And none of it has brought poor Nola any happiness. "There are two things in this world," she used to say, and laugh. "Both of them is money." It's not so funny any more.

The truth of it is she'd give all of that money, or most of it anyway, if she could have had Percy Valentine. But she couldn't, and she can't, and that's what bothers her. "Lord God," she told Miss Willie once, "if I could find a man who was half as good as him . . ." But he sits there in his law office, oh, late at night, sometimes after twelve, and everybody wondering. They used to tell tales on him. Some of them said he kept a nigra woman. And I guess Nola heard that, too. And maybe believed it. Maybe she called Miss Willie because that morning, in the post office, she ran into Percy Valentine. And he tipped his hat, and she asked him how his mother was. "Mama's getting mighty feeble," he said, or at least Nola said he said that. And she said, "Willie . . ." Miss Willie was listening. "Do you reckon when his mama dies . . . ?"

That's the way it was. Not only the women. Men too. Find a man who'll talk and he'll talk you half to death. Only you have to get him started. Like old man Borne. Old man Borne was mean; he'd whip a man as soon as look at him. Used to drink and cuss and raise all kinds of Cain. He was too mean to die, people said, and maybe they were right. He's eighty now. He sits out there under the china trees and whispers to himself, tells himself about the time he shot his wife's dog, Miss Lizzie's dog, because she liked the dog, the dog liked her, and he had to put a stop to that. Or about the time she burned the pan of biscuits and he made her eat them all, a dozen biscuits, and in front of company. Now he's sorry, they say. They say he'd like to take back some of the mean things he did, but he can't. Miss Lizzie's dead and he's all alone; there's no one to trim his hair or to cut his fingernails. Or even to talk. Except Miss Willie. She used to pass his house and sometimes she'd go and sit with him.

"Good evening, Major Borne," she'd say. They called him Major. Sometimes he wouldn't speak to her. Because he was mean, I guess. But she'd keep talking, and after a while he'd say, "Now, who are you?"

"Willie Mangham, Major Borne," she'd say. "You know me."

"Oh, yes," he'd say, "I know you." Then he'd commence to talk. "One time Lizzie . . ." And he'd look at her suspiciously. "You never knew Lizzie, did you?"

Yes, she said, she knew Lizzie.

"That's right. She was your age . . . just about your age . . ." The Major was confused, of course. Miss Lizzie was Miss Willie's father's age. But, anyway, she let him talk. She never stopped anybody, once they started to talk.

I expect she heard about the time Frieda Lee Brumfield tried to hang herself. And about Edna Wyatt's baby, the one she said she picked up at the orphanage, all eyes, with Bubba Grimmett's chin. And the night Edna locked Bubba's mother in the upstairs room and called the law to her. Oh, Edna was a crackerjack! And about the Lusby twins. The Lusby boys were so alike their mother called Steve "Cleve" and Cleve "Steve," and their wives didn't know them apart. That's how the story went: in their younger days they were taking turns without the two girls knowing it. I expect Miss Willie heard, if not from Steve, from Cleve. They're both big talkers. And as to whether or not the girls would have had to know, I'm one of those who think they would.

These are just a few of the things Miss Willie listened to, and that anybody could have listened to, who was willing to take the time. It takes time, lots of time, to be the ears of the world. And the reason she listened was she wanted to write, and there's nothing wrong with that. At least, that's what she said. She was born to write. But (and this was the trouble, and she knew it, too) there was nothing she could write

52

about. She had never *done* anything. She was fifty then, and an old maid. She had never *been* anywhere, except as far north as Memphis and as far south as Panther Burn. She was born up there in that house, and she was pretty sure to die there. She had never *heard* anything. She was so particular. She was either inside fixing herself or outside fixing her yard —out there in the flower beds. She hadn't heard anything because she hadn't taken the time to listen.

Well, all this came to her. "There I was," she said, "sitting there at that typewriter, and I got to thinking, *If somebody would just listen* . . ." So she began to listen. It was slow at first. Nobody knew she was willing to. After a while they caught on. They talked a little bit more, and a little more. She heard a whole lot more than she had hoped to hear, and more than she could hope to use.

Well, in the excitement, nobody seems to remember who it was that found out she was writing a book. It might have been Frieda Lee, or Ouida Woods—she's been known to halfway listen while she talked. Whoever it was, they got the story out: all in an afternoon the town knew it, knew that she was going to write a book, and some said she had already finished it and sent it off, to have it printed, which was not the truth, of course.

Some of them tried to laugh it off. Lucy Pembleton did. No sooner had she heard Miss Willie was writing a book, or about to write a book, than she made a beeline for the telephone. "Hello . . . this you, Willie honey?" she said. "Willie, this is Lucy. Can you come over? I mean, right away?"

Miss Willie said she could. I expect she thought Lucy had done it again: fallen head over heels, and was about to fill her in on it. Anyhow, as quick as she could, she got there and plopped down on the sofa in Lucy's living room.

Lucy didn't waste any time beating around the bush. "The reason I called you . . ." she said. "I heard . . ." And here she laughed. "It's being talked around that you're writing a book."

For a minute Miss Willie just sat there. I guess she didn't know what to say. "Well," she said, "not exactly . . ."

"That's what I told them," Lucy said, and she laughed again. "Willie is not exactly writing a book, I said. Why, Willie never wrote anything in her life, unless it was a letter. And, I declare, I don't know who she'd be writing a letter to."

Miss Willie tried to smile, but it was hard to. After all, she had told Lucy, maybe not in those words, that she was born to write. "Well, the truth of the matter is," she said, "I *am* going to write a book."

Lucy looked at her. You ought to see how big her eyes can get.

"And I've just about finished the first chapter."

Lucy looked at her some more, and then she started to laugh. "Willie honey," she said, "for a minute there I took you serious. I said, Willie *is so* going to write a book. And I said, Now what you suppose she's going to write a book about? And then I remembered. I said, I declare, Willie's pulling my leg . . . Willie never wrote a book in her life. . . ."

"It's going to be twenty or more chapters," Miss Willie said.

Lucy was still laughing. She was laughing so hard that the tears rolled down her face, and when she tried to stop she almost lost her breath.

Nola was the maddest one. Here she'd been telling Miss Willie all these things in strictest confidence, and now Miss Willie was going to go and write them up. It was two days before Nola could get hold of her: everybody was wanting to talk to her, and, of course, she was keeping the pavement hot, going first one place and then another. All of them asking the same thing: "Is it true you're going to write a book?"

Nola didn't even ask that. By the time she got ahold of Miss Willie she figured that she was going to write a book all right, and she had a pretty good idea about what. "This book you're going to write," she said, "does it mean that much to you?"

Miss Willie was tired of talking and tired of listening, and not exactly happy with the way things had turned out. "I just don't see," she said, "why everybody's so upset over me writing a book."

"Listen, Willie," Nola said. "You know I'm your dearest friend. I'm just telling you this for your own good. There's been a lot of talk . . ."

"Talk!" Miss Willie said. "That's all I've heard is talk." And she put her fingers to her ears.

"All right," Nola said. "If you're not going to listen . . ."

The next time she saw Miss Willie, which was the next day, she started out by telling her how tired she looked. And she did, of course. Only Nola didn't have to say it. "What you need, Willie," she said, "is a trip someplace. I've been wanting to give you a trip. A surprise. Mobile. Bennie and I used to spend summers down on Mobile Bay."

Miss Willie shook her head. "It's mighty sweet of you," she said, "but I wouldn't know what to do in Mobile."

"Well, Gulfport," Nola said. "I know people who'd give their eyeteeth to go to Gulfport. And it won't cost you a cent. I'm giving you the trip. Because you're my dearest friend. Don't you understand?"

"I just want to write," Miss Willie said.

"If it's money . . . money don't mean a thing to me. You must need money for something. That house. Get it done over, inside and out. Anything . . ."

Miss Willie looked at her. Until then, I don't expect she knew how strong they felt. "Nola," she said, "if you're trying to buy me off . . ."

"Buy you off!" Nola said. She'd been caught at it.

"Yes," Miss Willie said. "Because if you are . . ."

"Now, Willie . . ."

"You're wasting your time."

With that, I guess Nola figured the cards were on the table. "All right," she said, and she got up, as if to tell Miss Willie she could go. "How would you like somebody to write a book about *you?*"

That took Miss Willie by surprise. "Who?" she said.

"Well," Nola said, "aren't you?"

"Well, now," Miss Willie said, "some of the people in my book might resemble some of the people we both know . . ." And she smiled. "But there won't be a name that you would recognize."

That really started things. Nola told everybody, and everybody had his or her idea about keeping Miss Willie from writing that book. Some of them wanted to take it into court, but, of course, there was nothing to take, except Nola's word, and that was not enough. Some thought of this, and some thought of that, and finally they decided that the thing to do was to send some of the men to call on her. Bubba Grimmett, because of all the talking Edna had done, and Cap Brumfield, because of the talking Frieda Lee had done, and Charley Love, who had done some talking himself (and who, though Cap didn't know it, was the reason Frieda Lee had tried to hang herself).

That was two Saturdays ago. They drove up there in Bubba's car and they found Miss Willie out in the yard, out there in her flower beds, where she was spending more time now that there was no one she could listen to. "You gentlemen want to see me?" she said.

So they sat there on the porch and Bubba told her what they had come for, only he didn't do a very good job of it. Smooth as Bubba is. He hemmed and hawed, and if Cap Brumfield hadn't made him stick to the subject, he'd have been off again, telling how Edna found that baby at the orphanage, and them knowing better. Finally he said, "Miss Mangham, we're asking you to give this up."

"Give what up?" Miss Willie said. She knew, of course, but she made out otherwise.

"That book," Bubba said.

"The girls are pretty upset," Cap said.

"Yeah," Charley Love said. "I never saw 'em so upset."

"Well, I don't see . . ." Miss Willie said, and she started to get mad all over again, "I don't see what this has to do with me writing a book."

"Well," Cap Brumfield said, "the girls seem to think so."

"Maybe . . ." said Charley Love. He was always putting his foot in it. "Maybe if you'd let us see what you're writing . . ."

Miss Willie looked at him real hard. I guess she had trouble keeping her tongue in her head. "No," she said, "I couldn't do that."

For a minute nobody said anything. Then Bubba spoke up. "Miss Mangham," he said, "I'm going to come to the point: the girls don't want to be wrote up."

That really got next to Miss Willie. "You mean," she said, "those things Edna told me about you getting her PG and making out that baby . . ."

Bubba's face got red.

"You ought to be ashamed of yourself."

"You going to let her talk to you like that?" Cap Brumfield said.

"You, too," Miss Willie said. "Telling Frieda Lee you were deer hunting, and all the time . . ."

"Now, listen," Cap Brumfield said. "No use getting personal."

I guess Charley Love figured he'd be next, and Cap would know what Frieda Lee had been doing while he was off hunting deer, or at least pretending to. "Come on, boys," he said. "We don't have to listen to that."

So they got up and marched down the steps and across the yard without ever looking back. They were getting in the car when Miss Willie called to them. "And you can tell the girls," she said, "*I am going to write my book.*"

She was as good as her word. The next day Ouida Woods, who lives next door, heard that old typewriter of the Manghams going, and when she stood a certain way she could see Miss Willie, there in the parlor, typing away. She's up there now, typing away. And Nola has closed her house and gone to live on Mobile Bay, and the others that Miss Willie used to listen to just walk around, walk past her house, hearing that peck, peck. All except Lucy Pembleton. Lucy stays close to home. No one sees her any more. And no one has heard from her since she ran that ad in the county paper saying nothing Willie Mangham writes about her in that book is true.

A
Tribute
to
The General

She had been in Richmond only once before, and that was in 1909, the year before The General died. She had gone with him when he went to address a Grand Encampment of United Confederate Veterans, and all across Virginia, sitting there in the chair car, The General was quiet. Sometimes he puffed at his cigar, but mostly he looked out of the train window, out onto the streets of Petersburg and the plains below Richmond, and when she said, "Billy," he didn't seem to hear. Maybe he heard. Maybe he heard the little boy who came up to him in the train station and said, "General, that charge you led . . ." Because that charge he led was now a part of history. If he hadn't led that charge, Lee would have had the men to turn the enemy's flank. If he hadn't led that charge, all those young men would not be dead now and all those widows would not be telling those stories on latticed galleries. But there were those who blessed The General's name and who said that because of his attack Lee was able to hold the field, and that was why The General looked out of that train window, and why, standing before the men in that abandoned hall, he wept. Not only because he was old, for he was in his seventies, but because that attack had settled nothing: if he had attacked sooner—or if he had not attacked at all—Lee might have turned the enemy's flank, and if Lee had turned the enemy's flank, his army might have won a smashing victory. And if that . . . The General wept for a succession of ifs and might-have-beens and probablys.

She did not know that then. She knew only that the war, and one day in the war, and a single hour, had broken his life in two. She would never know that other part of it. And so she watched The General (how grand he looked in his faded uniform!), and when he had finished and the men stood, she stood, and then he came down off the platform and moved among them, down to where she was. "Boys," he said, "my lady." And one of the men said, "Old Billy's lady." And they gave a cheer for her.

Miss Jenny remembered that, and those other cheers, long after Billy's passing. And she remembered when the cheering stopped—the vacant years when she lived alone in the house The General built for her and when it seemed he was forgotten, except by the young professors who sometimes came to ask if they might see his letters, which she had kept, or the letters to him, which she had also kept. Angry letters. Bitter letters. Soldiers refighting old battles.

And then, long afterward, when she was in her seventies, it suddenly began again. A letter came, inviting her to speak

before the United Daughters at a meeting in Montgomery.
She went. She spoke briefly. "I am deeply honored, and I
know this honor you bestow upon me is your tribute to The
General . . ." It became, at last, a kind of ritual. Each year,
once a year, sometimes twice, she performed the ritual.
Alone, and always by train, she went, as she had come now,
at ninety-one, to the gallant city of Richmond. But no longer
alone, for at eighty-three her ankle gave way and she fell
and broke her hip, and at eighty-four she declined an invita-
tion to appear before a patriotic group in Nashville because
the hip had never mended properly. After that, Maudy Bea
accompanied her. "My eyes," she said. Her ears, too. A
gentle woman. A gentle colored woman who lived in the
house with her and rode the train with her, who helped her
to her seat and sat there next to her. And a friend.

And so they rode into Richmond, the aged lady and her
colored nurse, to perform again (perhaps for the last time)
the solemn ritual. The ladies were in their flowered dresses.
They were always at the station to welcome her, and they
gave her a corsage of sweet peas, which Maudy Bea took
and thanked them for.

"She don't hear well," said Maudy Bea, and she heard
that. She asked the ladies if this was the Richmond train
station, and one of them said, "Yessum, it is," and she asked
them if this was the train station that was here when she and
The General were here, and the ladies asked her when was
that. "Let's see," she said, and she had to think a while,
"nineteen-o- . . . nineteen-o-nine." And Maudy Bea told
her, "No, mam, Miss Jenny, I don't expect so."

Later, when they were seated in the hall where the Sons
and Daughters of the Confederacy had gathered, she asked,
too loud, if this was the hall where The General had given
his address, and the ladies around her began to look at her,
and Maudy Bea put one finger to her mouth, and she asked,

61

"Did I say something wrong?" Maudy Bea shook her head.

She didn't want me to come here noway, she thought. She's afraid I'm going to fall and break that hip again. Or my bladder's going to get too full and she's going to have to take me out of here. Then she remembered how thirsty she had been. Maudy Bea hadn't let her have a swallow of water since along about supper. Or was it dinner? "I got to have me some water," she said.

"It won't be long and I'll get you some water," said Maudy Bea, and she tried to whisper it.

"Well, if it won't be long," she said. She wondered why she had come here anyway. Out of some long habit. Memphis and Charleston and Jackson and Savannah. Because The General was gone and she was all that remained, all there was left of that legend. In a little while the man on the platform would stop talking and the regent or the vice-regent would take his place, and whoever it was would begin to talk about The General and about The General's wife, and then everybody would stand up and somebody would give the Rebel yell and start to sing "Dixie," and then Maudy Bea would help her to her feet and would whisper to her, "Wave. Wave now, Miss Jenny," and she would lift one arm and wave that little handkerchief, that little handkerchief that Billy had worn into battle.

She knew whose handkerchief it was. Billy's first wife's— the girl he married back in Tennessee, a girl with hazel eyes and an oval face and weak lungs. She died at twenty-three, the first year of the war, and he grieved for her through the war and for a long time afterward. Maybe forever. In those letters there was one from her, written in a childish hand, the year before they were married. "Dear William, I send this by the boy Ned. You must come here Sunday if you can. Pa has bought me a bay mare and you can ride the little mare with the white feet, back to that place we found . . ."

The place they found. Miss Jenny closed her eyes and saw that place, the way she had imagined it: a pine-straw path, a clearing in the woods, two horses, the riders leading them.

"The General's a fine man," her mother said, "but thirty years makes such a difference." It did not matter. She had known, from that evening on the gallery, that she would marry him. "Miss Jenny," he said, "I know it's presumptuous of a man my age to hope . . ." To hope! She was twenty-six; The General was then in his fifties. Already he had fought that fight a hundred times, the way Longstreet had his, because they had lost and because losers are bitter. Already he had spoken in a hundred cities. And in other cities there were other generals. If Johnston had moved sooner . . . if Beauregard had pursued the enemy . . . if Jackson had lived . . .

"All those boys," The General would say. He would say that, and in his eyes she could see the smoke of distant battles. "The decision was mine. No one else's. The orders left it to my discretion."

"Billy . . ." she said.

"Do you think I was wrong?" he would say.

And she would tell him no. "No, Billy."

He went on fighting that fight, and she went on believing he was right, or at least that he was not wrong. They traveled about the country, sometimes when she wished that they were home again, and The General spoke, or marched, or listened for the cheers, that moment when suddenly, out of a crowd, a voice would cry out, "God bless you, Old Billy." But there were other moments, when small boys came up to him in railroad stations, or when the parade wended its way past a house and a porch and a woman in mourning who turned her face from him. And that night, late into the night, The General would sit there in the hotel room and she would try to talk to him. "Billy, I bet you were

63

handsome as a young man." For he was. She had seen him in the photographs, a captain then, and his hair not white, and his eyes not blurred with smoke. But that was someone else, someone back before his memory. "What was it like?" she said.

He never answered her. Likely he was remembering that woman on the porch, her face away from him, or the woman whose handkerchief he had carried into battle. Her name was Rose. ROSE, BELOVED WIFE OF WILLIAM. And that child, and that child's grave, there beside the river. INFANT SON OF ROSE AND WILLIAM. The soldier's son, and the son of a mother with weak lungs, who died in two days and who was buried there beside a river. The General's brother took her there. His younger brother, who believed his legend as she did, but who stayed on that farm and never fought. And when he had taken her there, to that graveyard, because she wanted to go, he rode her up the hill a ways to where there was a chimney of brick, and he told her, "That was it."

And she said, "The house?"

"Yes," he said. "The Yanks burned it."

And she remembered what The General said, maybe one of those nights in one of those hotel rooms, after one of those parades. "Sometimes," he said, "I think we lost because we wanted to." Did it have to be, she thought, so terrible?

The man on the platform was eulogizing President Davis and the room was warm and for a few moments Miss Jenny dozed. She was dreaming of that place she never saw when a touch on the arm awakened her. "Is it time?" she said. She opened her eyes. Maudy Bea nodded.

One of the ladies was on the platform now and she was talking about The General. The old tributes. The spirit, the gallantry. And as she talked, Miss Jenny remembered him, his freckled hands, the mole on his chin and the smell of his cigars, but mostly his eyes, the smoke of distant battles. And she remembered how he looked there on that bed, as if, by some touch of the hand, those years had all been rolled away. She could hear his breathing. "Eh . . . eh . . ." And once she whispered, "Billy." And she saw him go, and thought again, Did it have to be so terrible?

They were standing now. They were singing "Dixie," and someone gave the Rebel yell. On the arm of Maudy Bea she rose, very slowly, remembering her broken hip, and carefully, before she remembered that she had drunk no water since the night before. Her throat was dry and she licked her lips. She could hear the cheers, so loud. Then she could hear, above the cheers, Maudy Bea telling her to wave. And so she waved, and she kept waving, and wondering, what it had been like, that time she never knew, before the fighting and the cheering, and wishing she had known him then, and had a son by him, and even that her name was Rose, buried by a river.

$\mathcal{A}$
Summer
$\mathcal{M}$emory

I suppose I must have seen Cousin Caroline twenty times or more in the years before that summer, but always at a distance—sitting upright and stiff under the steering wheel of the Lincoln automobile she bought the year that I was born; going into the post office, on those rare occasions when she did not send Marianna instead, to fetch the mail; once at church, down in front, gloved and veiled and watched by all who had grown used to the sight of the empty Armstead pew. I remember how she arose when the sermon was over and before the closing hymn was sung, and left by the side door, and I remember thinking what a great big woman she was, and how mean she must be: I had never seen her smile.

She was not big the way some people are big; she was what we used to call big-boned, and the clothes she wore were of another day and age—down to her ankles and high on her neck, some of them brocaded, and all that I remember a peculiar shade of lavender I had never seen before and have never seen since. I have heard my father say she was pretty once, the way the Armsteads were pretty, he said, and then he always added a little sadly, "Caroline was my favorite cousin." But the Cousin Caroline I knew could never have been pretty. Her eyes were too pale and much too wide apart; her nose was long; her face was as oval as an antique brooch and white white, moth white.

Twice I remember being spoken to by her, and both times from a distance. Once at Grandma Munday's funeral, which was the year I had my tonsils out, and Cousin Caroline was there—at the funeral, I mean. She carried a parasol, and she broke a sprig from one of the wreaths and held it in her hand, and when the service was over she stopped and said something to my father and pointed her parasol at me. "So you're Dudley's boy," she said. Her voice was loud. "Well, you don't favor Dudley much." I buried my face in my mother's skirts, heard my mother tell her I was shy. The other time she spoke to me was a long while after that. Billy Hughes and I had been down to the Bogue and we cut across her place and she was sitting on the gallery. Marianna, too. The two of them were playing cards—double sol, I guess. Then Billy showed himself and she caught sight of him from the gallery and hollered, "Who's that there in my hedges?" I started to run, but Billy said no, so we both came out and she said, "What are you boys doing in this yard?"

Marianna spoke up. "That's Mr. Dudley's boy, Miss Carrie. The little one." Marianna knew me from seeing me around, and I knew her from seeing her around.

"I don't care who he is," said Cousin Caroline, getting up

from her card game. "You boys get out of here and don't come back."

The funny part was, we were close kin to Cousin Caroline and we lived just down the road a way. As far back as I can remember, she lived there alone in that ugly yellow house with the dormer windows and the lightning rods. With Marianna, of course, to keep her company. It was the old Armstead house, and my father remembered when Cousin Caroline's people lived there and when the shutters were open and when he and she and Marianna played hopscotch under the china trees. Marianna was brought up from the plantation by old Mr. Armstead to nurse his only daughter; she was just a girl herself. She was sent back to the plantation the year Cousin Caroline went away to school. But the year old Mr. Armstead and his wife took sick with fever and died in the same room, Cousin Caroline came home. She buried her mother and father out in the family graveyard behind the house, and she closed the shutters, and she sent for Marianna to come. All of this was long ago, before my time. For me, there was only Cousin Caroline and Marianna and the ugly yellow house. There was also the Lincoln automobile, which was bought the year that I was born and which must have cost a pretty penny, Mother said. To which my father replied, "Well, if anybody can afford a Lincoln automobile, Caroline can." My father could never have afforded such an automobile. Our lands were the same, made rich by the same floods, but we depended upon ours and our cousin down the road permitted hers to grow in cockleburs. She was what we called, what we would have called that summer, a woman of considerable means.

Even now, the memory of that summer is incredibly real yet strangely unreal. It was an August afternoon. I was playing in the side yard, and for some reason (I suppose I heard the car) I came around the house to see. There was

Cousin Caroline, all dressed in lavender, coming up the walk. My father must have seen her too, for before she could reach the steps he was down in the yard to meet her, and I heard him say, "Caroline, this *is* a surprise."

"How've you been, Dudley?" I heard her say.

"Oh, pretty well." He shook her hand. "Now, if this weather . . ."

"It *has* been hot," she said. And then, almost in the same breath, "I'd like to have a talk with you, Dudley."

"Why certainly, Caroline." He helped her up the steps. "You mind sitting here on the gallery? It's cooler here on the gallery."

"It's a matter . . ." There was something in her voice— it could be that she spoke too fast, or maybe I imagined it. "I have to talk to you in confidence."

My father laughed. "Well, you came at the right time," he said, "if you want to talk private. Ella's in town." My mother always went into town on Friday afternoons. "Here. Have a seat here in the swing, Caroline."

"How *is* Ella?" she said.

"Oh, Ella's fine," he said.

But I doubt that she heard. "Dudley, I came to you . . ." I heard her say, and then something else I couldn't under-stand. She was in the swing and her back was to me. So I got down on my hands and knees and crawled up under the front steps. I could hear all they said from there. She was telling him something about Marianna, only she didn't call her that. She kept saying "my nigra woman." And once my father said, "You mean Marianna?" And she said, "Yes." And then I knew why she had come: Marianna was dead.

"Four days ago," she said.

And my father said, "I'm sorry to hear that, Caroline." He meant it, I could tell.

"I thought if you could come . . ."

My father scuffed his shoes against the floor. "In this heat . . ."

"Oh, I've got her underground," said Cousin Caroline. "I buried her shallow. But I want her moved."

"Who did you get to bury her?" my father asked.

There was a silence. When Cousin Caroline answered, her voice was low, but not too low for me to hear. "I buried her myself," she said.

"You buried her?"

She must have nodded.

"Caroline . . ."

"But I want her moved. I want her in the family plot."

My father got up. He walked to the edge of the gallery.

"There's only one place left," she said. "You know the place between Uncle Nathan and Cousin Genevieve . . . ?" All at once her voice was loud again. "There's no more room, Dudley."

I know what he must have been thinking. I was thinking it too: Cousin Caroline's crazy, lost her mind. "You know I'll do what I can," he said.

The swing chains creaked. "I know you will."

"I'll send two of my nigras over in the morning . . ."

"No," she said quickly. "You mustn't do that."

"Why not?" he said.

"You don't understand," she said. "I came to you because . . ."

My father kind of laughed. He said, "I never dug a grave in my life, Caroline—and I won't, so long as I got nigras to do it."

"Dudley . . ."

A sudden roll of thunder shook the house. It's going to rain, I thought, and then they'll go inside. But Cousin

Caroline sat there. She said something about Marianna and he said something about Marianna and then I heard him say, "You *what?*"

"Yes," she said.

"Why didn't you tell me?"

"Because," she said, "I never intended . . ." The swing chains creaked again. "Dudley . . ."

"When did you say this happened?"

"Four days ago," she said. "Monday afternoon." And then she told him how it happened. She had told Marianna to wash the soup tureen. "You know," she said, "it was Grandma's soup tureen, and I had told her to be careful with it. Nigras are never careful with things." She was ready to go out. She was in the back hall and she had picked up her umbrella from off the rack when Marianna came up to her and told her what she'd done. Broken that soup tureen. "I guess I lost hold of myself," she said. Before she knew what she was doing she had brought that umbrella down across Marianna's head.

"You hit her?" my father said.

"Yes," she said. "Maybe twice, I don't know. She grabbed her head and she kind of fell against the door, but she didn't say anything. She didn't even cry out. Maybe she did. I tell you, I was so . . ." Some of what Cousin Caroline said I couldn't hear. Then she said, "I don't see how. Maybe it was her blood pressure. You know she had high blood pressure."

"When did you find her?" my father said.

"An hour or so later," she said. "I was so upset I went out and walked around the yard. When I came back in I went up to her room. Her door was shut. I asked her if she was all right. She didn't answer me. So I opened the door . . ."

"And you found her there?"

"Yes. I tell you, it was a shock."

"I guess it was." My father cleared his throat. "How old was Marianna?" he said.

Cousin Caroline must have thought for a moment. "Sixty-eight," she said. "She'd be sixty-nine her next birthday."

"I didn't know she was that old," he said.

"She was Bicky's oldest child."

My father said, "She was a good nigra."

"Yes, she was a good nigra," Cousin Caroline said. Her voice was the voice I remembered: the game of cards, the funeral. "She was the only nigra I had, and I don't know how I'm going to make out without her. Somehow."

"Who else . . ." my father said, "who else did you talk to, Caroline?"

"No one else," she said. "Dudley, I came to you . . ."

"You haven't . . . ?"

"I told you," she said. "I came to you because I want her moved. I want her in the family plot."

For a minute my father didn't say anything. Then he said, "You know this puts a different light on it, Caroline."

"How do you mean?" she said.

"I mean . . ." Another roll of thunder shook the house. The smell of rain was in the air. "You've got to go into town and tell them what happened."

There was a terrible quiet. I was thinking: *go tell who?* Cousin Caroline knew. "But it's none of their concern," she said.

"I'm afraid it is, Caroline. The law . . ."

"Law?" She got up out of the swing. "Marianna was my nigra woman, Dudley."

"Tell them what you told me," he said. "Marianna was a good nigra . . . you wouldn't have hurt her for anything. But you got mad . . . you lost hold of yourself . . . anyhow, she was old . . . she died off in her room. Tell them what happened, Caroline."

"No," she said.

"You've got to."

"Dudley . . ."

"I'll go with you."

I heard her walk across the gallery toward the steps. My father must have caught her by the arm. For a moment she stopped. "You're my own kin," she said. "You're my only kin and I came to you for help . . ."

"Don't you understand, Caroline?"

"I understand," she said.

"I'll go with you if you want me to."

"Do as you please, Dudley."

"I'll get my hat," my father said. I heard the screen door slam shut and open again, heard her footsteps and then his going down the steps, heard him say, "There's nothing to worry about, Caroline. Everything's going to be all right." I sat very still until I heard the sound of an automobile starting. Then I looked out one side of the steps and saw Cousin Caroline's Lincoln turn in a wide semicircle of dust. She was sitting upright and stiff under the steering wheel; next to her my father sat, upright and stiff too, and talking, I could tell. Saying everything was going to be all right. And as I watched, the rain fell, settling the dust where they had been.

Ten years before, or even five, Cousin Caroline could have walked into the county courthouse and told them she killed her nigra woman and walked out of there without a bond. Maybe she could have done it then, that August afternoon, if she had done the right kind of talking. But Cousin Caroline did the only kind of talking she knew, I suppose: Marianna was her nigra, and if Marianna was dead, then that was her concern. The law was something the Armsteads never recognized, because they themselves had been the law in the days before the railroads came through their plantations and the towns and cities grew from the gins and country stores that they had built. I know this because my father took me with him to the trial; that long, hot day we sat in the little courtroom on the second floor and listened while the State went through its ritual. I think my father was shamed by the sight of his favorite cousin brought to trial, tried by a jury of twelve ordinary men, good men perhaps, but without the blood and breeding of the Armstead men. The courtroom was crowded. The word had gone around: they're bringing Miss Caroline to trial for manslaughter; and those who had known her from a distance, as I had known her all those years, came now to satisfy their curiosity. If she understood that, why they were there, she gave no sign of it. Once, as the day wore on, my father took her a cup of water from the cooler and she shook her head. That was the only recognition she gave anyone.

It was like nothing I had seen before, the trial, and I watched it all—the judge and the prosecuting attorney and the jury, each of them and all of them, and the prosecutor's witnesses. But it was her I watched most of all. She sat there inside the railing, in front of us and a little to the side, in one of those high-backed chairs the lawyers use. Her face was powdered and white. Her hands were gloved and she kept them in her lap. She had come to court alone, without a lawyer there to fight her case; she declined the offer of the judge to appoint her one. She had no questions to ask, or none that I recall, as one by one the witnesses were heard. I remember how many witnesses there were, though I doubt there were as many as there seemed, and I remember thinking: poor Cousin Caroline, she'll never have a chance. There was the sheriff and the sheriff's men, three or four of them, and the coroner and his assistant, and the doctor who said a bruise such as the coroner described could have caused the death of Marianna Washington. There was also the old man who said that once he had gone to the Armstead house to fix a pump and he overheard Miss Armstead and her nigra woman in an argument. "Would you say it was a heated argument?" the prosecuting attorney asked. And the old man said, "Yes, sir, it was a heated argument." There must have been others I forgot. And after each of them had testified, the judge would lean forward and say, "If you have any questions, Miss Armstead . . ."

And each time, the courtroom would get suddenly quiet, hushed to hear what she would say, which was always, "I have no questions."

Once I thought she would—have questions, I mean. One of the sheriff's men was in the witness chair, and we all got quiet when he told how he was present when the body of a nigra female (that's the way he said it), aged about sixty as well as he could tell, was dug up from a shallow grave under the china trees. "It was wrapped up in a quilt," he said, "as well as I could tell."

"And tell the jury what you did with it," said the prosecuting attorney.

"I didn't do anything with it," the sheriff's man said. I was listening to him—we all were—but I was watching Cousin Caroline. "The coroner, he examined it and told us to bury it back, but deeper. It was pretty badly . . . the heat and all. So the nigras we brought along to dig it up buried it back in deeper ground." I thought I saw her mouth grow tight, pull a little to one side. This time, I thought, she'll have questions to ask. But she didn't. She just sat there, pale as death, and when the judge asked her if she had any questions, she shook her head.

I remember the excitement when we found out she was going to take the witness chair herself. "You understand, Miss Armstead," said the judge, "that you are not required to testify, that if you testify, you do so of your own free will."

I heard my father whisper, "Don't do it, Caroline."

"I understand," she said, getting up.

At that, there was a lot of commotion, a lot of stirring around, and the judge rapped for quiet, and rapped again, but it was still noisy until Cousin Caroline took the witness chair. Then there was a funny quiet, a quiet you knew might break into noise again. I forget if there was an oath or not, though there must have been, but I remember the first question the prosecuting attorney asked, because to me it was a foolish question, I suppose. "Miss Armstead," he said, "did you know the deceased Marianna Washington?"

She looked at him. We waited. "Yes," she said.

And then, remembering that he had not established who she was, he said, "Would you please state for the court your full name?"

"Caroline McCauley Armstead," she said.

There were other questions after that: how long she had lived in this county, how long she had known Marianna Washington, questions such as that, and then the question we had waited for. The prosecuting attorney looked down at his notes and then up. His voice was low. "Miss Armstead, I want you to tell the court . . . did you on or about August fourth of this year, in this county, strike the said Marianna Washington?"

The quiet was broken only by the whir of fans overhead. "I did," she said.

"And will you tell the court how this happened?"

She looked at him.

"In your own words," he said.

"There's nothing more to tell," said Cousin Caroline. I saw her mouth grow tight again. "Marianna was my nigra woman. I had told her to wash the soup tureen. I had told her to be careful with it. When she came and told me she had broken it, I was furious. I never intended hurting her, but I was furious."

"And you hit her?"

"Yes."

"And will you tell the court," said the prosecuting attorney, "where you hit her and what you hit her with?"

"My parasol," said Cousin Caroline. Someone in the courtroom laughed. My father looked around; I must have looked around, too, and then back at her. "I was going out and I had my parasol. She put her hands to her head, but she didn't say anything. Later I went to her room and found her there."

There were other questions after that, some I've forgotten and some I haven't. Cousin Caroline was in the witness chair for most of an hour, but by then I knew it was all right. When she said, "Marianna was my nigra woman," I knew it was all right. So the prosecuting attorney gave his summation and the judge turned the case over to the jury. We watched them go out the door and up those steps out of sight, and we sat there, each of us wondering, I suppose, what Cousin Caroline was thinking. In a little while my father went inside the railing and stood there next to her and leaned over and said something I couldn't hear. She never looked at him, and so he came and took his seat again. Then the jury came back in, and one of the men read the verdict, which was "Not guilty," of course, and the judge congratulated the men and rapped on the bench for quiet. "You've heard the verdict, Miss Armstead," he said. "You're free to go now."

Without a word she arose and walked through the swinging door and down the aisle and out the back of the courtroom, all the people behind her, and some of them saying how glad they were. I doubt if she listened, or, if she listened, that she heard. I ran ahead too, because she was my cousin, and my father ran ahead and caught up with her just as she was getting into her Lincoln down by the row of trees. "Is there anything I can do, Caroline?" I heard him say. And above the noise of the crowd I heard her say, "Nothing, Dudley." Then she started her automobile, and the last I saw of her she was headed up the street and out of town, faster than I had ever seen her go.

I remember my father saying, "What will become of Caroline, you suppose?" It was natural to wonder that, after the years she had spent alone in that ugly yellow house with only Marianna to keep her company. The answer was not long in coming. Within a week of the trial, a nigra man who had gone to sell her pullet eggs found her there. He ran for help, and we were the nearest help. I was there before my father was. I ran the back way, and up to the graveyard fence, and when I looked inside I saw her there. She had fallen face down in the shallow hole; her hands were locked tight about the handle of the spade. Then my father came running up, and into the graveyard through the gate and over to where she was. "It's Caroline," he said, as if I didn't know. He stood there looking down at her. Then he turned to me and said, "Run on home. Run on home before you see something you oughtn't to."

I ran, but before I ran I looked once more, at Cousin Caroline, at the shallow hole and the stones on either side: NATHAN ARMSTEAD (and the dates); GENEVIEVE McCAULEY (and the dates). Then I ran, and I kept running all the way home.

The next morning my father took his nigras there and they finished digging the hole that Cousin Caroline had started. And he had them do the strangest thing. They dug up the body of Marianna Washington and buried it there, in the family plot, between Uncle Nathan and Cousin Genevieve. And out under the china trees they buried Cousin Caroline. The stones are still there.

The
Return of
Andrew
Ferengold

One summer evening Andrew Ferengold left his wife, his home, and the deceptively comfortable life that he had lived for almost twenty years. It happened so suddenly that Andrew could never explain it all himself, beyond the fact that at five minutes after five he had closed his office and started in the direction of the café across the street. His intention, if intention it was, was simply to have his customary glass of beer before going home to Evelyn. Yet at a quarter after five he found himself alone on the highway on the edge of town, presumably waiting for a bus. When the bus came (it was five twenty-five, he noted by his watch) he stepped aboard, paid the driver the fare to the farthest point, and sat back to consider the facts of the most remarkable day in his life.

That he was leaving Evelyn did not give him great concern; after all, he had contemplated leaving her for almost twenty years. But the thought of leaving had been rather like a childhood promise—the Christmas present that never comes, the journey that is never taken. Now the present had come, the journey was being taken. What did concern Andrew Ferengold that summer evening was that there was no why to his leaving. Not only was it unpremeditated but it was unprovoked. There had been no quarrel. Evelyn had not sought the affections of another man, and certainly he had not sought the affections of another woman. His practice was good. His finances were never better. Then why was he going away? He could not say, and he found that fact disquieting.

At another time he might have said. Eight years before, when Evelyn confessed that she had never loved him, never would, he might have left knowing why he was leaving and with no thought of coming back. Or twelve years before, the year the doctors told him she could never bear a child, he might have left her then. She had known that when he married her; he was sure of it. Yet she had pretended that one miraculous season she would conceive, would carry his child to the ninth month and, in pain, deliver it. He might have left then hating her. But even this deception was forgiven, if not forgotten, and he had seen his yearning for a child for what it was: a desire to project himself into another time.

Now, on a summer evening, he was projecting himself into another place, and without a reason he could find. This was the thought that caused him such concern. There were other thoughts. Where would he go? What would he do? How does a man of forty-three begin his life again? Can he, in fact?

The answer to the first of these questions was the easiest of all. He rode the bus to the farthest point and he traveled on from there. He traveled by road and by rail. He walked the streets of cities he had never seen, towns whose names he had never heard. Sometimes he stopped, for a day, two days, perhaps a week, but always he was driven on by a savage kind of restlessness. Once he spent two weeks in a little town in sight of both the mountains and the sea, thinking this might be the place. But the people acted strangely there: they watched him, and he knew that he must go on to a place where the people did not watch one another, where they were beyond love and hate and even friendliness.

There was such a place, and there he stopped. Time had passed. Summer had passed into fall, and winter into spring. And now, Andrew asked himself, what was there for him to do? The answer to this he found in the classified advertisement columns of the newspapers, but only after he had undertaken countless jobs, useless jobs that merely paid his lodgings and bought his meals and cigarettes. He considered practicing again; that was discarded when he enumerated the obstacles which might be encountered in a city such as this—he had no friends, no clients, no funds to lease the necessary office space. He was not a member of this bar. And besides, he had grown somewhat weary, he admitted now, of the practice he had left behind. It had ceased to be the challenge that it once was, in those first years of his life with Evelyn.

And so, in his new life, Andrew Ferengold read the newspapers and took what jobs he could and was glad for them, and one day he answered an advertisement that took him to a second-rate hotel. It was a hotel where the guests and the clerks exchanged meager pleasantries and where those who simply could not pay their bills were given an extension of another week. Despite the fact that they were spoken of as guests, a great many of them had spent their lives within the hotel, and some had come there under other managements.

The job that Andrew Ferengold was offered, after the usual interview, was night clerk, lodgings free and a starting salary of forty dollars a week. He took the job reluctantly. He did not like the hotel and he did not like its guests. Or, to be more exact, he was aware of the fact that he probably would not have liked them in his other life. They were such people as he would have met only professionally, in his office or before the judge's bench—men who might have come to him to swear adultery and women who had spent their alimony checks on cheap and hopeless drunks. But here in the lobby of this second-rate hotel he made a strange discovery: that all of them shared something he shared, too, but did not understand. At last, it occurred to him that he was lonely, that each of them was lonely, yet without the capacity to comfort another in his loneliness.

Sometimes he thought of Evelyn, the summer evenings in their youth, the whispered talk under the china trees, and then, without really wanting to remember, the talk that evening on the darkened porch. The swing chains creaked, and out in the yard a locust sang, and Evelyn talked, talked, about anything and everything but what he wanted her to say: that she had been to the doctors that afternoon, that they had told her she could never have a child. He knew. He had gone to them behind her back. It was like some terrible game—the postponements of months and years, the empty reassurances, now this final postponement of Evelyn's, this talk of hers.

But he had waited long enough. "You can't, can you?" he said suddenly, angrily.

The darkness screened her face. Whatever the expression there, whether of desolation or dismay, he could not see. "I was sure I could," she said.

"Were you?" he said. He would force it out of her. "But they told you you can't?"

She waited a moment. "Yes."

"Then why didn't you tell me? Didn't you think I'd want to know?"

"Andrew . . ."

"Didn't you think I cared?" he said.

She did not reply at once. The swing chains creaked; out in the yard the locust sang. "If you had known . . ." she said, "if you had known would you have married me?"

He looked at her, or rather, toward her in the dark, wondering what kind of woman she could be to ask him that.

"Would you?"

"Yes," he said. That was the irony. There were other ironies: the futile precautions they had taken in those early years to see that there would be no child; the selfish lovers, guarding the love which they later found—which he later found—was not even love.

"Andrew . . ." She spoke his name as if from memory. "I'm disappointed, too, you know."

Disappointed? he thought. Was that all? Disappointed?

"I suppose we could adopt a child," she said. "Lots of people do."

"Evelyn . . ."

"I know," she said. "I know you blame me . . ."

"Don't be ridiculous."

"You're sorry you married me, aren't you?"

He did not answer her.

"Aren't you?" she said.

He closed his eyes and thought of leaving her, how it would be. She would sit here on this porch and she would talk and the swing chains would creak and she would not even know he was gone. The words she spoke, she spoke from memory.

"You shouldn't have married me, should you?" she said.

And the words she heard, they had all been spoken, too. *I love you, Evelyn. I've never loved anyone . . .* "No," he said, "I don't suppose I should."

She laughed. She got up out of the swing laughing and he heard her laughter as she crossed the porch, and even afterward, the echo, like the sea noise in a shell.

These were the things that Andrew Ferengold remembered. He remembered the darkened porch and the talk and the laughter, and he knew now why he was here, why he stayed at this hotel he did not like, among these guests he did not like. They were waiting, all of them. He was waiting, too. But for what? If there was someone he could ask . . . if there was someone who could make the waiting bearable . . .

There was. Her name was Mrs. Reno Sims. In other circumstances he might not have noticed her. She was like any one of a hundred women who sit in hotel lobbies on winter evenings, overrouged, overdressed, handsomer than most, perhaps. Yet there was something about her that attracted him. Her eyes. He could see it in her eyes—a certain weariness. From the waiting, he thought. She would sit until he dimmed the lights. Then she would get up and cross the lobby and she would pass the desk on her way up to her room. And always she would stop. "Is there any mail for me this evening?" she would say.

He would tell her no. For he came to learn without looking (though look he did, to keep appearances) that the only mail Mrs. Sims received was a check which came to

her on the first of every month and which she folded care-
lessly. "That wasn't what I was looking for," she would say.

And he would say, "I'm sure it will come tomorrow."

"If I get a Special Delivery . . ."

"I'll call you," he would say.

One evening, quite impulsively, Andrew put a letter in
her box. He had written it himself, and this is what he said:

*My dear Mrs. Sims: Would you consider it presumptuous
of me to ask if we might sit down sometime and talk? I
want so much to talk. Sincerely, Andrew Ferengold*

"Why, Mr. Ferengold," she said when she came to ask
about her mail and found his letter there. "You've taken me
by surprise . . ." And disappointed her, he saw. For his
letter was not the letter that she sought. "You say you'd
like to talk?"

"Yes," he said.

"About what, might I ask?"

"There's so much," he said.

"For instance?"

"For instance, why I'm here, why you're here."

"Oh," she said, and smiled. "But, of course, we must talk
sometime."

And so they did. It was difficult at first, for him, for both
of them. Later it was easier. He did not find in Mrs. Sims an
end to his loneliness, nor did she find in him an end to hers,
but neither had expected to. She still inquired about her
mail; he sometimes thought of Evelyn. Nevertheless, their
relationship, for that was what it was, was almost all that
Andrew Ferengold had hoped. Perhaps not all. There was
still, he found, a barrier—the suspicion that she knew a
great deal more than she would say. Yet she said a great
deal. She, too, had had another life: a husband who loved

her wisely but not too well and a daughter she was sure would one day write to her.

"You're fortunate," he said.

She looked at him.

"You have a child."

"Yes," she said. "I have a child."

"Is that the letter . . . ?"

"Yes." Her voice was hesitant. "I don't understand," she said. "I went away one day and not from that day to this have I heard . . ."

"Why did you leave?" he said. He had asked her that before. She had never answered him.

This time she did. "Oh," she said, "for a lot of reasons, I suppose."

"Such as . . . ?"

"You'd have to know Mr. Sims. Mr. Sims was twenty years my senior."

"And that was why you went away?"

"No," she said, almost apologetically. "I mean, there were other reasons. It happened suddenly. Those things do."

Yes, he thought, those things do.

"*You* . . ." she said. "Why did you?"

"Well, to tell the truth," he said, "I don't know either."

"You don't know?"

"No," he said.

She laughed uneasily.

"Have you . . ." He held the question on his tongue. "Have you ever thought of going back?"

"You mean . . . ?"

"I mean, to see . . ."

"Whether I was missed?"

"Yes," he said. "I suppose that's what I meant."

"No," she said quickly. "I never wondered. I never wanted to know."

"I have," he said. He thought of Evelyn. "If I ever do go back . . ."

"You think it would be any different?"

"No," he said. "But at least . . ." He looked at her. "It's the waiting."

"Yes," she said, "it's the waiting."

"For what?" he said. He had wanted to ask her that. But no, he thought: the barrier.

"For whatever . . ." Mrs. Sims smiled. "You know how long I've been here? Sometimes . . . I've seen it . . . sometimes for the smallest thing."

He knew what she was thinking: a letter.

And so he waited, and Mrs. Sims waited, and her letter never came. She was wearier—he saw it in her eyes, and wondered what she saw in his. Still they talked, until there was nothing left to be said, and sat.

"You never wondered . . . ?" he said.

"No," she said.

"If I could go back . . ."

"Don't," she said. "You'd only . . ."

"What?"

She did not answer him. Light faded at the window. They sat.

"Only what?"

"When you've been here as long as I have . . ." she said.

And he thought: when I've been here that long . . .

One afternoon he left. One afternoon when he had not meant to go at all he sat there in his room and remembered what she said. And before the evening came he left.

Andrew Ferengold's return was not what he imagined it would be. The streets were deserted in the summer sun; there was no one out for him to see—or to see him, for that was what had bothered him, how he might observe without being observed, what care he must take to keep from being recognized. It was not the recognition that he feared. He rather liked the thought of Cal McLean or Owen Richardson coming upon him on the street—the look on their faces when they saw that it was Andrew Ferengold, come home again, and after all this time. But he did not want to have to talk to them, tell them where he had been and why he went away. They would say, "Poor Evelyn . . ."

Poor Evelyn. He wondered what emotions the sight of her might stir. They *had* been man and wife. They *had* sat down to the same table, gone to bed in the same bed, and for almost twenty years. What if he should come upon her suddenly? What would she say? What would he say? He had considered the possibility. Or one of them (Owen, Cal McLean) might go to Evelyn, tell her they had seen him here. He had considered that possibility. But when he set foot upon the pavement of the town again he at once discarded it. The streets were deserted in the summer sun. He could walk to his heart's content, and without the fear of being recognized.

So he walked—past the courthouse and the street of stores, along the row of cedars by the Baptist church. There was no direction to his steps; he merely walked, and having walked the other streets he came at last to the street where he and Evelyn had lived. He felt an odd excitement as he approached the house, the green yard and the hedges by the walk. His muscles tensed. For a moment he looked, half expecting to see Evelyn come out onto the porch. But there was no one there. The door was open behind the screen and inside, he knew, beyond the living room, beyond the hall, Evelyn lay there on the bed, the fan turned full on her. Perhaps she was sleeping. Perhaps (he dared to think) she was even in her sleep remembering. Then he caught sight of the swing; the sound of swing chains echoed in his ear. His steps quickened. He passed the house. He reached the corner, turned, looked back.

Now there was the café where Andrew used to go and sit, a typical small-town café with the usual tables and chairs and the row of stools, and there he would go on summer evenings such as this. It was a pleasant place to sit and reflect upon the business of the day, to drink his customary beer and look through the plate-glass window at the street. And so today, as Andrew walked the streets, he found himself in front of this café. He knew that he should not go in, that Mr. Angelo would be on his stool beside the coffee urn, that Cal McLean and Owen might be there. Before he could reason with himself he had pushed the screen door open and made his way inside. There was no one at the counter. Mr. Angelo was not beside the coffee urn. A boy came out of the back and Andrew thought for a moment that it might be Mr. Angelo's son. But it was no one that he recognized.

They spoke. Andrew sat down at the counter. "A beer," he said.

The boy looked at him.

"Draft," he said, remembering his customary glass of beer.

"We don't serve draft," the boy said.

"No draft?"

"Jax . . . Bud . . . ?"

Andrew frowned and told him Jax. He looked around him. The café was much the same as when he went away. The fans were turning overhead, the pin-ball machine was still on TILT, the sign on the wall above the phone said WHERE WILL YOU SPEND ETERNITY? Where indeed? he thought. He looked at the phone. Again his muscles tensed. He remembered how he had passed the house. If he had stopped . . . if he had gone up on the porch . . . but he had turned the corner, wondering. How would it have been? He would have knocked . . . no, he would have opened the screen and gone inside . . . perhaps called her name. *Who's there?* she would have said. And he would have said, *It's me, Evelyn.* She would have come up off the bed. He would have had to face her there—and that, he knew, was what he could not bring himself to do. There was another possibility. He could call her on the phone. Again he looked at it.

The boy brought his beer, set it in front of him.

"Didn't you . . . didn't they use to serve draft here?" he said.

"When was that?" the boy said.

Andrew smiled. The thought of it saddened him. "Oh, a long time ago," he said. He sipped his beer and looked out at the street. He saw a man he did not know come out of the barbershop and get into a car; there was a woman next to him. She had dark hair. She reminded him of Evelyn. "Do you mind if I use your phone?" he said.

"Sure," the boy said. "Over there." And he pointed.

Andrew got up and made his way between the tables. He picked up the receiver and when the operator asked him, "Number, please?" he spoke from memory. He could hear her ring. He started to hang up. She rang again. Someone lifted the receiver at the other end. A woman's voice said, "Hello . . ." It was a voice he knew. He tried to speak. "Hello . . ." His heart was pounding wildly in his throat. "Hello . . . hello . . ." He replaced the receiver on the hook. For a moment he stood there. Then he went back to the counter and his beer.

"You couldn't get your party?" the boy said.

"No," he said. Perhaps Mrs. Sims was right. He should never have come back. *It's the waiting,* he had said. And she had said, *Yes, it's the waiting. For what?* he said. *For whatever,* she said. *Sometimes for the smallest thing.* Andrew looked at the boy. "Do you know," he said, "a Mr. Ferengold?"

The boy said, "No." He shook his head uncertainly.

"You never heard of him?"

"I could have." He did not seem interested. "Why? He lives here?"

"He used to," Andrew said. He finished his beer and sat there looking at the street. In a minute he would get up and go outside; he would walk to the highway on the edge of town. He would not be coming back again. Evelyn would never know that he had walked past the house, that he had called her on the telephone. And he would never know . . .

"You want another beer?" the boy said.

"No," he said. He laid the change on the counter. He got up. He walked to the screen door and looked out. Then, with the weariness of long waiting, he turned and went back to the phone. He picked up the receiver and when the operator asked him the number he spoke from memory.

"Hello . . ." It was her voice.

He tried to say, "Evelyn . . ."

"Hello . . ."

"Hello," he said. It was a voice he did not recognize.

"Who *is* this?" she said.

And he said, "Evelyn . . ."

"Andrew?"

"Yes, Evelyn," he said, "this is Andrew." He could feel the heartbeat in his throat.

"Well, for goodness' sake," she said, "you don't sound like yourself."

Aren't you going to ask me? he thought. Aren't you going to ask me where I've been and whether I've come home again?

"You going to be late for supper?" she said.

Late for supper? he thought.

"I need a loaf of bread."

He wanted to say, "I've been gone, Evelyn. Aren't you going to ask me where I went?" But suddenly he knew— why he had gone away and what he had waited for. *To be missed.* Simply that. *To be missed.*

"Would you pick me up a loaf of bread?" she said. He took the receiver from his ear. He could still hear her voice. "Andrew . . . ?"

"Yes," he said.

"You won't forget the bread, will you?"

"No," he said, "I won't forget the bread."

He put the receiver back on the hook. He stood there by the plate-glass window, and across the street he saw Owen Richardson come out of his office and get into a car. He wanted to run out of the café, out onto the street, to say, "Owen, it's me . . . Andrew. I've been gone, Owen." And he did get to the door. But he stopped there, and he watched Owen drive away.

"Did you get your party?" the boy said.

He turned. "Yes," he said.

"That name . . ." the boy said. "What was it?"

What name? he thought. And then he remembered. "Fer-engold."

"Yeah," the boy said.

"You never heard of him?"

The boy shook his head. "No," he said, "I never heard of him."

Then Andrew laughed. He laughed there in the café. He laughed as he walked to catch the bus on the highway at the edge of town. And as the bus pulled away he laughed some more, at the thought of Evelyn, waiting for her loaf of bread.

The
Rarest
Kind of
Love

They crossed the Bogue bridge and headed down the moonlit road that once had been an Indian path, past the mounds, and Troy remembered: he had climbed them as a boy, had stood at the top; they were tall then, and in the distance he could see the town. Yet he knew that if he climbed them now, in the moonlight, they would have grown small and the magic would have gone from them, the smell of the sassafras roots. "Now it's your turn," he said.

"Well, there's nothing much to tell," she said. "Married. Divorced. Your mother always was a fool where men were concerned." In the dashboard light he could see that she smiled, and her smile was almost the way he remembered it, the old Deedie Ringgold, extravagantly beautiful. Where had it gone, then? All those years, he thought. And always that face, that smile, there in the dashboard light. "No," she said, "I have nothing to show for it. But it was painless. Thank God for that."

"You haven't changed," he said.

She laughed. "I'm a few years older."

"And wiser?"

"No wiser."

No, he thought, if you had it all to do again . . .

"But you know," she said, "everybody tells me that. When I tell them I have a boy twenty-nine . . ."

"Thirty," he said.

"Are you *really?*" she said, and again in the dashboard light he saw her smile and that night came back to him. That ridiculous night, there on the gallery. He was twelve, or maybe thirteen. It was one of those Christmases when he was off at school and he had come home for the holidays. But he came home to an empty house. And a note. I'LL PICK YOU UP AT SIX, the note said. WILL EXPLAIN. And he sat there alone in the house that afternoon and wondered: explain what? At six she came, and blew the horn in front of the house; she was smiling, and they drove this road, past the mounds, the way they had tonight. To the Ringgold house, the house where she was born and where his father courted her, there on that gallery. And there on that gallery she told him. *Your father and I . . . well, Troy*, she said, *you know A.C. and I never got along. We're two different people. And . . . well*, she said, *to make a long story short, we've decided we can't live together any longer.* He stood there and he thought: to make a long story short. And she said, *This doesn't mean I don't love A.C., or that A.C. doesn't love me. And, of course*, she said,

*we both love you. You're our only child. And we've decided
. . . that is, our lawyers have decided . . . that for a
while it would be best for all concerned . . .* For all concerned, he thought. *If you spent summers with A.C. and
Christmases with me.* He wanted to cry, but he would not
dare to let her see him. *Now,* she said, *won't that be fun?*
And he said, yes (he was still holding the glass earrings
he had brought her for Christmas), that would be fun.

They passed the Fauver house and she said, "Laura
Fauver . . . I always hoped you and she . . ."

Laura Fauver, he thought. It was all so long ago.

"She was such a pretty girl. And she was just crazy about
you. You remember? And you were crazy about her. What
happened?"

"Oh," he said, "after that summer . . ."

"She married that Baxter boy. What was his name?"

"Bo."

"Bo Baxter."

That summer, he thought. They had gone for a swim
in the moonlight, down past the Bogue bridge, and they
wound up at the hunting camp. It was locked, but he knew
where his father hid the key, and they built a fire, though
it was summer and there were fireflies at the window
screens. They had gone there once before, that Christmas
he was home from Vanderbilt, and he had meant to make
her then. Not like the girls on the back seat of the car in
Nashville, painless and quick, but with pain and with joy,
because she was Laura Fauver and the thought of her ex-
cited him. So he begged her please, until it became a
crazy thing with him. *I love you,* he said, because what was
love then but a throb, a thrust; only now he was sure of
it. *Troy,* she said, and laughed. *Please, Laura,* he said.
And she laughed again and said, *What am I going to do*

with you? But that night it was different. They came in wet from the swim and they sat there on the porch and they were nineteen and so much was back of them. It was the end of something, more than summer, and they knew but did not speak of it. Then he tried again, that game, that oldest ritual. *Troy,* she said, and he knew. It was in her voice. He slipped out of his trunks, and she her bathing suit, and they stood naked in the moonlight there, white and motionless. Outside, the trees were still and the air was hushed. Later he would remember that. The air was hushed. And they came together in the moonlight there.

"I had hoped you and Laura Fauver . . ." His mother laughed. "But I'm not going to worry about what might have been. If there's one thing I've learned . . ."

If there's one thing you've learned, he thought, it's never to be touched by anything.

"I still can't believe it," she said. "When I picked up that phone this afternoon and heard your voice . . . you don't know what it's been like, Troy . . . never a word, not even a card . . ."

He looked at her. The wind was in her hair; she put her hand to it.

"And if it took *this* . . ." she said.

He knew what she meant: if it took his dying. If it took A.C.'s dying to get him here.

"He sent for you?"

"Yes," he said. "He had them call. He said he thought I ought to come home."

"Home?" Her fingers tightened on the steering wheel.

"I still say it." He smiled. "I still say home."

"Well, I can tell you," she said, "it was never home to me. I went there as a bride in 1931 and it was never home to me. Oh, he's your father," she said, "and I know that. And he's a sick man. But the truth's the truth. Deedie's going to tell the truth."

He smiled and thought: Deedie never knew the truth.

"Is it cancer?" she said.

"Yes," he said.

"But if they operate . . ."

"They're not going to operate."

"I'm sorry," she said.

No, he thought, you're not. Not really. "It's a funny thing," he said. "He gave me everything I ever wanted."

She laughed. "Except the one thing."

"Some people can't," he said.

"Oh, I loved A.C.," she said. "I was wild about A.C. He was my first love. But he killed my love. He killed your love, too. You shouldn't hate him."

"I don't," he said. "I don't hate him." And again his father's face came back to him, that death's-head, those eyes, the plea in them: *Troy.* But there's nothing Troy can do, he thought. Except be there when it happens. Maybe I should have stayed, he thought. But the nurse said . . .

"I hope," she said, "when it's over . . ."

When it's over . . . , he thought. A man lives sixty years, and he dies, and all you can say is, *It's over.* And he thought: I shouldn't have left. Even if the nurse said . . . it could happen any time.

"I hope," she said, "you'll stay a while."

"I'm afraid I can't," he said.

"Troy . . ."

"I have to get back." And he thought of that cemetery on the road to Idlewild. It was on his left. He saw there were blocks of it. A city of stone. No, a borough of stone. For the cab raced on, and still he saw it there: ugly, terrible, obscene. As if . . . yes, he thought, that would explain it all—the faces on the subway, in the Eighth Avenue bars, peering out of the windows of those brownstone apartments on Seventy-second Street. And this, he thought, is where those faces go, this great elephant burial ground, and one day it will reach as far as Idlewild and beyond, down to the ocean.

"I never thought . . ." she said. "When you left, I thought that in a year or two . . . how long has it been, Troy?"

"Nine years."

"Nine years," she said. "It seems that you've always been gone from me. You remember when you went off to military school? You were just a little thing . . ."

I never wanted to go, he thought.

"You don't forget," she said.

No, he thought, you don't forget. *This.* The moonlight and the Indian mounds and behind them the Bogue bridge and ahead the Ringgold house, those galleries. *This.*

Now they were turning up the gravel drive, through the grove of cedar trees. "Well, there it is, Troy . . ." And she laughed. "Does it look like you remembered it?"

He looked to see: that great white house, those endless galleries, the splendor of some planter's dream. You could smell the land from there, the smoke from the burning woods, and the dust, and you could imagine, on nights like this, that the land ran on and on, on to the river and beyond, that there was nothing to limit it. "Bigger," he said.

Inside it was the same: the preoccupation with size. Rooms thirty feet square. Ceilings thirteen feet high. Those mirrors he had looked into. And he looked again, as if, he thought, to see the image of a boy reflected there.

"We've closed the upstairs," she said. "Huntley and I

lived up there. You remember Huntley. I had it all redone. Brought down an interior decorator from Memphis. Oh," she said, and laughed, "you wouldn't know the place."

"And Aunt El?" he said. He remembered Aunt Ella Ringgold, his mother's aunt, the daughter of a sawmill operator out of Yazoo City who came here as a girl, the bride of Will Ringgold, and who never belonged in this house, they said.

"Aunt El keeps a room at the back of the house," she said. Perhaps she was remembering the time he ran to her, ran to Aunt El and put his head in her lap and smelled the darning gourd and the thread and the smell (he imagined it was the smell) of a dusty sawmill town. "I know she'll want to see you."

And yet, he thought, she outlived all of them: Will Ringgold; Will's brother Hal, his grandfather whom he had never seen; and his grandfather's second wife, his step-grandmother, Miss Ione, who spent her last years in a Memphis nursing home. "Yes," he said, "I want to see Aunt El."

"If I had known you were coming . . ."

He smiled. "I hardly knew myself."

"You can sleep down here tonight. And tomorrow I'll get Leola . . . we still have Leola . . . I'll get Leola to open up one of the rooms upstairs."

"No," he said, "I really can't stay. My things are at the hotel."

"But that hotel . . ." she said.

"It was near the hospital."

"Well, I know . . ." she said. "It's there, close to the hospital. But I wish . . . and I know you wouldn't want to stay at A.C.'s place. He tried to sell it, you know. Some people who work up at the oil mill. But they tell me . . ." She laughed. "They tell me when they went in there they changed their minds—there were whiskey bottles all over it."

He thought of that house, the only home that he had known, and how he had waited there that December afternoon until his mother came for him.

"Now you go sit down," she said. "I know you must be tired, that plane trip down and that ride on the bus from Memphis. You sit there and I'll fix us a drink."

"Nothing for me," he said.

She looked at him quizzically.

"Don't worry," he said, "I haven't given it up. It's just . . ." This afternoon, he thought, and that face came back to him. *Troy* . . . That tired hand reached for his. *They called you?* And he said, yes, they called him. And his father said, *I didn't want to bother you, but you know* . . . He knew what his father was thinking: I didn't want to bother you, but you know I got cancer. *How you been, boy?* Fine, he said. *That's good.* Then his father said, *Troy, there's something I want you to do for me.* And he asked his father what. *They won't let me have any whiskey. Get me a little whiskey, boy.* Well, if they don't want you to have it . . . , he said. And his father started to cry. *I got to have some whiskey, Troy.* And he thought: that's a little thing to ask; a man is dying and he wants a little whiskey and that's a little thing to ask. So he went out and went up to his room at the hotel and got out the bottle of Scotch and took it back with him. *Scotch,* his father said, and made a face. *I never liked Scotch, but at a time like this* . . . Troy laughed. And then his father saw it was funny, and he laughed a little, too. *At a time like this,* he said, *you can't be choosy.*

"A.C.?" she said.

"I suppose that's it."

"Well, then, you need a drink," she said.

"Some wine," he said.

"Yes," she said, "some wine. Ceremonial wine." She tried to laugh. "This *is* a ceremony, isn't it?"

"Deedie . . ."

"Call me Mother," she said.

And he thought: I've never called her that.

"You know," she said, "when you were a little boy you called me Deedie and A.C. A.C., and then for so long a time," and she laughed, "you didn't call us anything."

"Have you seen him?" he said.

"A.C.?" She poured the wine and handed it to him. "No. The reason I didn't go in . . ." she said. "I know A.C. would have been glad to see me, but I didn't want to be depressed. You know how your mother is."

Yes, I know how my mother is, he thought.

"Things like that depress me. And A.C. . . . well," she said, "A.C. *was* my first love. This other marriage . . . Huntley Dunn . . . it wasn't the same. . . . It never is the same." She looked away from him, out through the door, out beyond the gallery. "When do they say . . . ?" And then back at him. "How long?"

"It could happen any time," he said.

"That soon?"

"Yes," he said.

"Maybe you should have stayed. I shouldn't have insisted."

"The nurse said . . ." *Do you think it's all right?* he said. And she said, *His pulse is good. He could last another day or two.* "But I can't stay long. I want to stop back by the hospital."

"And you want to speak to Aunt El."

"Yes," he said.

"We'll do that now."

He got up and followed her.

"Aunt El is really quite remarkable," she said. They

passed through the hall into the rooms beyond and down a narrow passageway. "She's eighty-three, you know . . ." There was a door. "Aunt El?" She opened it and they went into a room where an old woman sat in a high-backed chair before a game of solitaire. "Aunt El, look who's here."

The old woman looked at him.

"It's Troy, Aunt El."

"Troy . . ." she said, and she smiled. "I declare . . . come here, boy, and let me hug you."

He put his face against hers and smelled that long-ago smell, of a gourd and thread and a dusty sawmill town. "Aunt El," he said, "you haven't changed . . . you look just the same."

She laughed. "I'm eighty-three."

"Eighty-three?" he said.

"Yes, I am." And she laughed again. "I declare . . . you children sit down."

They sat there in the room with her.

"I was just asking Deedie the other day. I said, 'Deedie, don't you ever hear from Troy?' And she said . . ."

"Aunt El," his mother said, "Troy came home because A.C. . . . because A.C.," she said, "is not doing well."

"Oh?" she said. "I'm sorry to hear that."

"You know he has cancer."

"No, I didn't know. And I'm sorry. A.C. . . ." The old woman laughed. "He was crazy about Deedie. Used to spend more time here, I expect, than he did at home. And Deedie was crazy about him. Weren't you, Deedie? Those young people . . ."

"Aunt El," his mother said, "Troy lives in New York."

"New York?" she said. And he knew what she was thinking: that's a long way from a sawmill town. "Well, tell me . . ." she said. "All about yourself. Did you bring your family?"

"Aunt El," his mother said, "Troy doesn't have a family. He never married."

"Never married?"

"Well, to tell the truth, Aunt El," he said, "I never could find a girl who would have me."

"Now," she said, and she laughed, "I know that's not so. A good-looking boy like you. Who does he favor, Deedie? Does he favor you? Both of you. A.C.'s eyes."

Those eyes, he thought: the plea in them.

"How old are you, boy?"

"I was thirty in July," he said.

"Thirty." The old woman laughed. "You children . . . I still think of you as children . . . you children don't remember the times . . . a girl was considered an old maid if she hadn't married before she was twenty. I was eighteen when Will Ringgold married me . . . brought me here in a horse and buggy. That was in 'ninety-eight. Why," she said, and she nodded toward his mother, "I remember when this child was born. She was such a pretty little thing. And her daddy . . . Hal Ringgold . . . your granddaddy . . . I never saw anybody spoil a child like Hal did this one. Why, Hal would go out and buy . . ."

"Aunt El," his mother said, "Troy wants to drop back by the hospital. We're going to have to go. I know he'll be back to see you."

The old woman looked at him.

"I'll see you again, Aunt El," he said.

"I wish you children wouldn't go."

"Well, we have to . . ." his mother said. "I love Aunt El," she said, when they had gone back in the other room, "but when she gets off like she does . . . sometimes I say, 'Now, Aunt El, if you can't talk about *pleasant* things . . .'"

Pleasant things, he thought. There was a picture on the table next to him. He picked it up.

"That was your mother," she said.

It had been taken in some studio. There was an arched trellis of roses, and she was standing there in the trellis, her eyes upon the camera, that smile: Deedie Ringgold, so beautiful, and (you could see it in her face) so absolutely sure of it.

"That was taken the year I married A.C. Your mother was so young then . . ." And he knew what she was thinking: so beautiful. "It's warm in here," she said. "Let's go out on the gallery."

"I really ought to be starting back," he said.

"What time is it?"

He looked at his watch. "A little after nine."

"One more glass of wine," she said. And she emptied the decanter.

There was a breeze on the gallery. It brought with it the smell of land and river, that ancient dream. "Here's where it began," she said.

"A.C.?"

She nodded. "We used to sit here . . ." And then quickly, as if she remembered that that was not a pleasant thing to talk about, she said, "And you never married."

"No," he said.

"How did you manage?" She laughed. "To escape, I mean."

"Oh . . ." he said.

"Maybe that's not the word."

No, he thought, that's not the word. You don't escape. You never do. And the smell of far cities filled his nose, dark streets, musty rooms. Those lies, he thought: *I love you, I love you, I love you,* those magic words that open all doors—and make escape impossible.

"Well," she said, "there must have been girls . . ."

"Oh," he said, "there were girls." But he was not wet from

the swim, and the moon was never so bright, or the air so still, or the trees so motionless.

"Well, I know you will," she said. "You'll find some girl . . ." She laughed. "She may not be quite all you wanted. But who is?" she said. "You might look all your life. Who is? And, of course," she said, "you're entitled to a few mistakes. Look at your mother. Your mother has made mistakes. This last marriage. And my marriage to A.C. A.C. was attractive. He could be terribly attractive. But I never should have married him."

"Why did you?" he said.

"Oh . . ." She made a futile gesture with her hands. "Why does anyone do anything?"

The phone was ringing. She went to answer it. It's for me, he thought.

"It's for you," she said. "I think . . ." Her face was pale. "It's the hospital."

He picked up the phone and he heard them tell him what he knew they would say and he said, "Thank you, I'll be there," and hung up.

She was waiting on the gallery. "A.C.?"

"Yes," he said.

"He's dead?"

"He died at ten after nine." He looked at his watch. "Fifteen minutes ago."

"Oh, my God," she said. "I don't think I can stand it." And she stood there in the moonlight crying.

Yes, he thought, you can stand it, and I can stand it, because he never meant that much to us.

"You should have been there," she said. "I shouldn't have insisted . . ."

"No," he said.

"Troy," she said, "he was your father . . ."

And he wanted me here, he thought. And I came. At least I came.

"A.C. and I . . ." There was an immense logic in her voice. "We never should have married . . . but, then, if we had never married, we wouldn't have had you. I wouldn't have had you, would I?"

No, he thought, you wouldn't have had me.

"And without you . . ." she said. He remembered how she had looked that night when they stood there on the gallery. He was holding the glass earrings in his hand and she was saying, *It would be best for all concerned . . .* "Because our love . . ."

He did not hear her. He was thinking of that night, and then, for no reason, of what A.C. had said: *At a time like this . . .* The breeze had died and suddenly the air was still. He laughed. *You can't be choosy.*

The
Great Day
of
His Wrath

Christ amighty, I don't guess there was ever a day like that one. Well, it was really a week. All week long those two little Shankle girls were going first here and then there, handing out those cards, and their daddy was out nailing up signs, and when he wasn't nailing up signs he was driving that old Packard with the loud-speaker on top. He brought that car with him when he came from over there around Crowder, and he drove people half-crazy playing those records of old Judge . . . what's his name? You know those records. He's been saying the world was going to end since Lord knows when. And people got tired of it. Miss Hattie Dyer said that racket was making her nervous, and

Mr. Polly McIntyre said if Mr. Shankle didn't get that sound turned down, and didn't get that car and that loudspeaker off the streets by nine o'clock, he was going to see to it there was a town ordinance.

Well, that stopped the Shankles for a while. I don't mean stopped 'em, because you couldn't stop the Shankles, but it sure slowed 'em down. Those little girls were careful whose door they knocked at, and when they got to Miss Hattie's house they crossed the street and tried the other side. They knew if they put one foot on her property she'd be out there quicker than you could say Jack Robinson. And not mincing any words. You know how she used to do the nigras. The nigras would go from yard to yard looking for greens. Those wild greens that grow along the walks. And they'd knock at your back door and say, "Miss, you mind if I get some greens?" Well, who minded if they got some greens, except Miss Hattie. "You touch those greens," she'd say, "and I'll call the law to you." She would have, too. And those nigras knew it. And those little Shankle girls knew it. One tried to hand Miss Hattie one of her cards once and she said, "Don't be handing me any of that." Like she didn't want to touch it. I don't guess she did.

Mr. Shankle had those cards printed. Those signs too. Jesus saves. Prepare to meet thy God. Things like that, and saying the end of the world was near, but never saying when. At least, not until that Saturday. Oh, Mr. Shankle was a funny one. Long face. Fish eyes. If he smiled he didn't let you see him. People used to say, "Don't look at him. That's what he wants." He could tell you the end was near and make you believe it. And if you ever let one of those little girls in your house . . . or their mother . . . Before you knew it, they had their foot in the door and they had pulled out some of that literature and had started reading it, or they had some records, and if there was a

Victrola in sight, which there generally was, they were over there playing it.

But that Saturday (I mean that Saturday it started) they were out on the streets earlier than usual. And Mr. Shankle was out in that Packard, with the sound going full blast, and this time he wasn't only playing those records; he was driving that old Packard with one hand and holding the microphone with the other, and you could hear it in his voice: "Brothers and Sisters, the end is at hand!" Not only was it at hand, it was going to be this Thursday. "Oh," he said, and he put on one of those records of a choir singing, "the great day of His wrath is coming, and who shall be able to stand?"

That attracted a good bit more notice than you would have thought. Maybe not at first, but later, when he had driven up and down the streets of the town a time or two, and when his wife had got her foot in a door or two, and those little girls had handed out a card or two.

The next time Mr. Shankle drove past the seed store Mr. Polly McIntyre came out in the street and motioned him to stop, and Mr. Polly said, "Now what's all this commotion about?"

"Brother McIntyre," said Mr. Shankle, giving him those fish eyes, "the end is near."

"You been saying that," Mr. Polly said, "since you come over here from Crowder three years ago, and I haven't seen it ending yet."

"Well, now it is," Mr. Shankle said. And he said he had spent the better part of his life just studying Revelations, when he wasn't carpentering, and he found something over in Ezekiel, or maybe it was Daniel, and he put some of the Scriptures together and came up with this: the world was going to end on the seventh day of the seventh month of the seventh year after the fulfillment of the prophecy. And between daylight and dark. "Oh," Mr. Shankle said, "it all comes in sevens." By then a crowd had gathered, and he showed 'em how it worked. He had it all down on paper. But not only that, he said. You could get it another way. And he showed 'em the other way. If you counted the blocks in the Great Pyramid . . .

"Daylight and dark?" said Mr. Polly McIntyre. "How's the world going to end in the daylight hours when, if it's daylight here, it's pitch dark in China? Now answer that one," said Mr. Polly McIntyre.

"I don't have to answer that one, Brother McIntyre," said Mr. Shankle. "Believe or don't believe." And he turned on that record of the choir singing and pulled off in the direction of the depot.

"You think it's anything to it?" some of 'em asked.

I guess even Mr. Polly was took in, though he wouldn't admit it. They say by the time that Thursday came he had got himself all worked up, and he came down to the seed store earlier than usual and stayed later. I guess a lot of people didn't let on they were bothered, but they were. Well, you can't blame 'em. The Shankles kept it up all week. That Packard must have drove a thousand miles, up and down those streets, like nobody'd ever said a word about nine o'clock. At half past eleven that car was still going, and Miss Hattie told somebody if she heard it one more time she'd scream, and the town marshal, who had got quite a few complaints, pulled Mr. Shankle over to the side up there near the water tank, and he says, "Friend, could you turn down your sound a little? You going to give Mr. Ollie Rheams another stroke." And Mr. Shankle said, "Marshal, I'll turn my sound down. I wouldn't want to give Brother Rheams another stroke, but at a time like this . . . I got to see that these children are ready. . . ."

Ready? By Thursday they were ready all right. Mr. Polly

McIntyre was down there at his seed store at four o'clock, dressed and ready, and Miss Hattie had her blinds drawn. I guess a nigra could have taken all the greens he wanted and got away with it. And I guess a lot of people who didn't really believe the world was going to end were nervous just the same. And it had to rain. Oh, it thundered and lightninged something awful, and then the rain started, and I guess that made 'em more nervous. Along about half past nine Mr. Phillips turned out school. None of the children were paying any attention anyhow. They just kept watching the windows, as if one more clap of thunder and the earth was going to swallow that schoolhouse up. Some of the folks didn't even send their children. If the world was going to end, they wanted the children there with them. Oh, later they wouldn't have admitted it. Lula Fox said she kept Pookie home with a red throat. That's not what I heard. I heard she took Pookie and the little girls down to the basement of the church and they spent all day there, and Pookie kept running out in the street and asking, "Is it ended yet?"

Well, by noon it hadn't, and the Shankles were still sitting in that old Packard out there on the baseball field. On those cards Mr. Shankle had printed up and those little girls had handed out from door to door, it asked everybody to gather at the baseball field. Maybe if it hadn't rained they would have. And there were a few cars there. The Brysons and the Lands. And old Jules McKee. I guess he was there, as much as anything, for curiosity. And the Shankles had that loud-speaker going. The music would play and then Mr. Shankle would read something from Revelations, or maybe Daniel, and then he'd say, "Let's all sing now." And they'd sing. The Shankles in their car and the Brysons in theirs, and there were some nigras who had gathered under a tin shed down at the other end of the field, and they were singing too. Oh, it was eerie, that singing from up at the baseball field, and the thunder, and Mr. Polly McIntyre coming out on the street every once in a while to look up at the sky.

Even old man Suggs was worried. I was up at the icehouse a little after three o'clock, and he said, "The Shankles still up at the baseball field?"

"Sounds like it," I said. You could still hear the singing.

"Well," he said, and he chipped me a fifty-pound block, "if it's going to happen, I wish it would."

Along about four Miss Hattie came out on her porch, and then one or two of the cars left the baseball field, and some of the nigras who had gathered under the tin shed began to wander off. But the Shankles were singing louder. That loud-speaker was on, and Mr. Ivy Adams, whose gin is up there by the field, said, "They ain't going to give up, are they?"

Not the Shankles. The closer to dark it got, the louder they sang. Then, along about five, the wind started to blow. It didn't last long but it blew some of the leaves off the trees, and rattled some windows, and that got people started again. Miss Hattie flew back in the house and Mr. Polly McIntyre started checking his cash register, watching the windows all the time, and I guess the Shankles thought they were ready to kiss the sweet feet of Jesus. Oh, they were ready, if anybody was. They had given away all their things, what things they had: all their clothes and all their furniture. "Because," Mr. Shankle said (he said it on the loud-speaker once), "we want to leave here as we came." Close to, anyway. They were going with the clothes on their backs, in that 1931 Packard. Can't you see that, the Shankles riding into heaven in a 1931 Packard?

Well, the wind stopped blowing and a little after six the dark came and the street lights came on and the Shankles stopped their singing. By then the others were gone. Mr. Shankle started the car. He sat there a long time with the motor running, and after a while he pulled off, going slow, off for that empty house.

But he never got there. Up there by the gin some of the folks had gathered. They had spent all day waiting for the world to end, and their children had stayed home from school all day and driven their mothers crazy. So they stopped the Shankles there near the gin, and they moved around the car.

"Now, Brothers and Sisters . . ." Mr. Shankle said. "I have read the prophecy . . ."

They didn't say anything. They just lifted the car up and tipped it over on its side, there on the street, the Shankles in it. You should've seen 'em come out of there, Mrs. Shankle out of one of the windows on top, which was on her side, and hollering for Mr. Shankle to bring the records, which he did, and those two little girls coming out of the other window, wild-eyed, looking all around, like they thought maybe *this* was the end of the world.

By then somebody had pulled the loud-speaker off, and somebody else had grabbed those records and started breaking 'em. "You come from over around Crowder," said Mr. Polly McIntyre. "Now go back there." The little Shankle girls were still trying to hand out literature, and Mr. Polly said, "And take these children. I mean it."

"The great day of His wrath . . ." said Mr. Shankle.

"And cut that out," said Mr. Polly McIntyre.

I guess Mr. Shankle knew he meant it. "Will some of you Brothers help me with the car?" he said.

Four or five of 'em stepped forward. They helped Mr. Shankle to right the car, and he got in and his wife got in and the children after 'em. "Brothers and Sisters," he said, "if you'll just give me a chance" (I guess he had the paper out) "to do some figuring . . ."

They weren't about to, of course. If the world was going to end and he had missed it by a day, they didn't want to know it.

"It may not be tonight . . ." With that, he started the car. And then the Shankles started singing. The last the town saw of 'em they were headed down the street past the baseball field and out on the road to Crowder. And still singing. I guess if it happened on that dark and lonesome stretch of road, they wanted to be ready.

Under
the
Blue Cup

When Mattie Silvers was young, before Mr. Billy disowned her for marrying a drummer, she collected cut glass. She was showy with it, too; cardboard boxes would come in from mail-order houses in Chicago and she'd open them right there in the post office, no pride at all. It's just another fad, people said, like dangly pearl earbobs, but she'll outgrow it. She kept on collecting, though, until the McIntyre parlor was filled to overflowing with her glass treasures, every one descended from that relish dish she won at a BYPU raffle.

When she took to bed with malaria, which she was apt to in July, Mr. Billy would bring her fever down with a new piece of glass. He humored her that way. But when he heard she was marrying Seab Silvers, heard it secondhand, he drew the line and dared Mattie to step across. He locked her in the parlor for thirty minutes and more, just begging her not to go through with it, for the Silvers were no-account, he said. He even promised to take her to Indianola on Saturdays for tapdancing lessons, and she had always wanted to go on the stage. At last, satisfied that she was paying him no mind, he smashed every piece of her cut glass and ordered her out of the house.

Why had she been willing to give up Mr. Billy and her glass treasures for a drummer, and a Buster Brown drummer at that? Well, she used to say it was because she loved travel; she loved the excitement of different towns and different people. Seab gave her those things. They traveled up and down the Delta on the *Peavine;* they stayed in elegant two-story boardinghouses with white ceiling fans; there were fish fries on Bogue Phalia and street dances at Lula-Rich, and there was the inexplicable magic of depot names, of going past and coming back again. The longest they stayed in one place was the summer Mattie laid up that ninth month, with nothing to do but endure her discomfort and drink ice water by the pitcher and wait. She was in labor two days and part of another, and in the cruel heat of an August noon the wait was over. The baby was born dead but she named him anyway—Billy McIntyre for her father, which was what she said she'd call her first boy.

Somewhere in the movement, in the confusion of train whistles, hellos and good-bys, she lost her grief. The memory of Billy McIntyre caught up with her only now and again on still, smoke-haze summer afternoons.

When the drummer passed out of existence in the Delta, Seab, like many another, settled down on a buckshot farm to raise cotton. It was a change that did not come easy for

Mattie. She missed the white ceiling fans, the lazy after-supper talk on boardinghouse porches. She had come to that restless time when women begin wondering, secretly, if what matters most in life has slipped away from them. Even flowers fade, and Mattie was aware of it. Her face, already narrow, had assumed a disproportionate narrowness. The light had left her eyes, and her mouth was querulous.

It was at this time in her life that it happened. It happened in the midmorning, up the Memphis highway, and by afternoon Mattie was back and the word had gone around. It was Seab who brought her back, in the pickup truck, with his mother riding on the side by the window so you couldn't see Mattie, except maybe the mottled yellow of her hair through the rain. Then Seab came back to town in a little while, and he and the deputy sheriff left the courthouse, going fast. People saw all the commotion. They ran hither and yonder telling about it. It was one of those things you read about, and they said anybody but Mattie Silvers would take straight to bed—not Mattie.

But she did, and while they were still talking. She crumpled up on the bed and said she'd never been so glad to see home; it'd been a long day and she was dog-tired. Actually it was a short day, a November day, and twilight came early, and the light that burned in Mattie's room burned dimmer as the night drew near. Outside, a south wind blew rain against the windowpanes. Quick gusts, caught beneath the eaves of the house, puffed the wallpaper where other winds had loosened it.

Close beside the bed Seab's mother rocked in a wicker chair. She was a frail old woman with eyes the color of smoke and a voice that came in whispered gusts like the wind. "Seab'll know what to do," she was saying. "Seab'll be back direc'ly."

Mattie propped herself on one elbow and felt between the feather mattresses.

"What you want?" the old woman said.

She drew out a capsule box. "Could you get me a swallow of water, please, mam?"

The old woman got up and left the room. She came back with a glass of water. "Here," she said.

"Thank you, mam." Mattie swallowed the capsule. "I been having a nervous condition," she said. "You know how it is when the change comes early. Now this. It wasn't like me to give strangers a ride."

Seab's mother took the glass and put it on the mantel.

"He couldn't've been more than twenty. No more than a boy. I says to him, 'Take the truck and go,' and he says to me, 'I don't want no truck, I want you.'"

"Don't try to talk," the old woman said. She sat back in the wicker chair.

"I try not to think about it . . ."

"You try not to."

"You believe in signs?"

The old woman nodded. "I should say I do. The Testament's full of signs."

Mattie sat up in bed, her face to the window. "Not a week ago I had a crazy dream. Dreamed I was running. I don't know from what, but I kept running. Then I threw my arms out and I took off. I flew. I never came to light."

The old woman quit rocking and leaned forward in the chair. "I used to have a dream book," she said. "Got it from one of those ladies selling hand lotion. You ever see a book like that, full of dreams?"

Mattie bobbed her head. "They say to dream of weddings is a sign of death. Or muddy water." Her eyes reflected the twilight outside the room, a reflection sharpened by the staccato beat of rain against the shingle roof. She reached out her hand and wiped the moisture from the window-pane, peering at the twilight and the gravel road beyond, shattered into cut-glass pieces by the falling rain. The gravel road ran zigzag through fields of bare cotton stalks, past McCullough's Store and Dredge Ditch 41 westward to the Memphis highway. Early in the morning she had traveled it in the pickup. Only the sun, a bloodshot eye on the far rim of the Delta, had watched her leave. The trip was not planned at all: it was sudden, like her sudden flight in the dream.

When she awoke that morning it was still dark but she could see by the luminous hands of the clock that the alarm had not gone off. There was a peculiar stillness about the room; even Seab's breathing, there next to her, seemed to come from another part of the house. She got out of bed shivering, slipped into her clothes, and went into the kitchen to make coffee. Daylight was beginning to show at the window. She pressed her face against the pane and saw the ground shimmer with dew. When the coffee was made she poured herself a cup, drank it standing up, rinsed the cup in the sink, and then tiptoed back into the room where Seab lay sleeping. Her hand shook as she turned the alarm to *Off*.

Outside, she walked across the yard to the pickup, got in, and started the motor. The sun was up and watching her, there between the chicken house and the barn and just above the thin line of willows by the Bogue. She raced the motor until smoke from the exhaust hung in the morning air. Then she drove westward down the gravel road. But the sun was faster, or else it had gotten a head start. In the mirror she saw it, watching her still, but higher in the sky. She pressed harder on the accelerator. Beyond McCullough's Store a white rooster chasing a hen ran the width of the road. She swerved to miss him, there was a bump, and the mirror reflected a white cloud of feathers that for an instant covered the sun.

When she reached the Memphis highway the sky was a sleazy blue. She waited for a school bus to pass, then turned northward behind the bus and the children waving to her from a back window. Their skinny arms drew fantastic circles in the air; their faces twisted into laughter and their lips shaped words she could not hear. But then the bus turned off onto a side road and there was nothing ahead but the white highway. The whiteness blinded her.

She had become conscious of a growing pain in the pit of her stomach. If I had something to eat . . . , she thought. She remembered that she had had her cup of coffee, the cup of coffee she always had, and she remembered the stillness of the room where Seab lay sleeping. Ahead she saw a filling-station café with a Morton's Salt sign for a front: *When It Rains It Pours.* She pulled off the highway and down onto the gravel in front of the café. A muddy terrier pushed his way out the screen door and stretched in the sunshine. She got out of the pickup and went into the café, took a seat at the counter facing a fat woman on a stool before the coffee urn.

"Morning," said the fat woman. "How you this morning?"

"Oh, pretty good," Mattie said.

"You want to see the menu?"

"Please, mam."

The woman pointed to the tin blackboard over the coffee urn. "Out of grits this morning. Got some nice fresh eggs, though."

Mattie studied it. "I believe I'll have some scrambled eggs," she said.

"Scrambled eggs," the woman repeated. "Muss up two back there," she called to a Negro girl peering from a door behind the counter.

"Could I have a glass of water, too?"

"Could you have a glass of water? Why, sure, you could."
The woman left her stool and came back with the water.
"Bound for Memphis, I guess," she said.

"Yessum." Mattie emptied the glass in one swallow. "That
was real refreshing."

"I don't guess I've been to Memphis two times since my
sister-in-law passed away. Her name was Ellen America
and she passed away three years ago this July—the Fourth
of July. That's why it comes to mind easy."

Mattie shook her head at the fat woman and said, "How
sad."

"Sad? Well, now, it wasn't really so sad. She'd suffered
a whole lot, and everybody said it was a blessing in dis-
guise."

"So many of our blessings come disguised," Mattie said.

"So many of our blessings," the woman repeated.

"I could tell you plenty," Mattie said. "You wouldn't believe the things I could tell you."

"I wouldn't believe the things you could tell me? I'll just
bet you I would."

"I could tell you why I left home this morning and why
I'm going to Memphis," Mattie said. She told the fat
woman. She told her Seab had been running around, with
one of the McCullough girls for all she knew; she could put
up with so much and no more, so she was going to Memphis to take a beauty operator course.

"A beauty operator course? That's something I always
wanted to do," the woman said. "I think you're being real
smart, sugar."

"I'll tell you another thing," she told the fat woman. "He
broke my cut glass. Every last piece, even my BYPU relish
dish, and I prized it most of all." She began to cry.

She was still crying when the Negro girl brought her plate of eggs, and she ate crying.

"You're just wasting those pretty tears," the fat woman called when she waved good-by. "Men are all alike. Nocount. You go ahead to Memphis and get him off your mind. Now you hear?"

"I'm going to try my best," she called back.

"That's right, sugar. You're going to try your best."

She drove away thinking of how the fat woman echoed what she said. It was like hearing her voice for the first time, like the time she made a record at the carnival and the record stuck and her voice kept saying *having fun having fun having fun* until she shoved the needle into a new groove.

Up ahead the sun's reflection moved with her, across the windowpanes of abandoned farmhouses, over the tin roofs of gins and barns and crossroad stores. Farther ahead thunderclouds began to crowd the blue from the sky. A boy in a blue suit was standing beside the highway thumbing a ride. She passed him. Then something about his image in the mirror caused her to stop. He ran and climbed into the pickup beside her.

"How far you going?" she said.

"Memphis," he said.

"I'm going to Memphis myself," she said. "I'm going to take a beauty operator course."

Her head felt light as heat rising from the concrete highway. It was the same feeling she had when she rode the merry-go-round and fell off onto the ground sick. Everything was two: a double exposure. The blue of the boy's suit and the blue of the sky became one, blinding her, until the shroud-gray thunderclouds blotted out the blue and rain fell with a frightening silence.

✿

Dark had come. Mattie turned away from the window. Her thoughts were worn thoughts, haphazard as a patchwork quilt and strangely frayed. She tried to remember laughter and days that passed too quickly, the smell of steaming cotton and dust, and long rides along the levee to Friars Point.

"As a girl I couldn't grow up fast enough," she said. "I'd swing and swing from a chinaberry limb so I'd grow up. One summer I grew two inches."

Her patchwork memory caught the chinaberry limb and the girl swinging from it, but the girl's face was an old woman's face and she hung there grotesquely.

"I used to run all over the Delta, one end to the other, and so dressed up . . . Mr. Billy'd say, 'Mattie baby, you beat all I ever saw for keeping your hips in the road.' "

She remembered Mr. Billy as an old man. Always he was an old man, and he smelled of medicine and laughed ha-ha when he talked. She remembered how he coughed before he got out of bed in the mornings and how he cheated when he played sol. He knew fourteen games of sol.

The rain had stopped but the wind still blew in gusts against the roof and Seab's mother rocked crazily. Someone was knocking at the door, calling, "Mattie Silvers, Mattie Silvers."

"Come in," she called back.

Three women came into the room and huddled together at the foot of her bed like sparrows on a telephone wire. They all wore wool coats and silk scarves and one carried a tin box. "We only heard a while ago," they said. "If there's anything we can do . . ."

"Seab'll know what to do," the old woman whispered.

The one with the tin box set it on the foot of the bed. "Here's a jelly cake," she said. "It fell, but I brought it anyhow."

"That's mighty nice of you," Mattie said. "Jelly cake is a favorite of mine." She ran her hand through her hair. "I know I must look a sight. But after what I been through . . ."

The three women huddled closer together.

"Wasn't it just awful? Did you ever hear of such an awful thing?"

One of the women said no and the others clucked their tongues in unison.

"He couldn't've been more than twenty. No more than a boy. I says to him, 'Take the truck and go,' and he says to me, 'I don't want no truck, I want you.'"

"Mercy me!" exclaimed one of the women.

"Oh, it was awful. I tell you, you never know . . ."

"You never know," the women said. One said, "We better run along and let you get some rest," and another said, "If there's anything we can do . . ." Then they broke apart and went out into the wind.

"That was mighty nice of them," Mattie said, "but don't you hate boo company? I'll bet I look a sight." She took the lid off the tin box and held it up in front of her. "When did Seab say he'd be back?"

"He'll be back direc'ly," the old woman said.

"You don't think he'll lose his head, do you?"

"Seab won't do nothing he oughtn't to," the old woman said.

"I hope he won't lose his head. You know how Seab is. I wonder what's keeping him."

"Now you lie still," the old woman said, "and I'll tell you a funny story when Seab was a boy." She laughed ha-ha, like Mr. Billy used to laugh. "As a boy Seab was plumb crazy about stray dogs. He'd go out Saturday mornings with his pockets full of cracklings and he'd come back . . . you should've seen the nigger dogs behind him. His daddy would get after him. 'Don't you go bringing those dogs home,' he'd say. One time . . ."

"Wasn't that the back door?" Mattie said.

The old woman listened.

"Yes, it *was* the back door. Seab?"

There were voices in the kitchen. Then Seab's voice, louder than the rest: "I'll be there in a minute, Mattie."

"Jesus God!" she whispered. "I wonder what kept him."

"Don't try to talk," the old woman said.

The door opened and Seab came into the room, His face was red and chapped from the wind and his eyes, pale like his mother's, squinted in the yellow light. "How you feel?" he said.

Mattie sat up on the side of the bed, one hand cupped under her chin. "Pretty good," she said. "What kept you so long?"

"I been up the highway with the deputy."

"Who's that out in the kitchen?"

He looked at his mother and then back at her. "They think they got the one," he said. "They want you to take a look at him."

"You mean . . . ?"

He nodded.

"You brought him here?"

"Maybe it's not him," he said. "Maybe it's somebody you never laid eyes on. They got to know."

"After what I been through?"

The old woman caught her son's hand. "Seab . . ." she said. "The girl's right. Listen to her."

"Don't make me, Seab."

"Mattie . . ."

"Tell them some other time," she said. "Tell them tomorrow."

He moved toward the door.

"Wait," she said.

He turned.

She lay back on the bed, pulled the blanket over her. "All right," she said.

The boy was handcuffed to the deputy. In the yellow light his hair looked wind-spun, like dusty cobwebs, and his skin soft and transparent.

"Howdy do, ladies," the deputy said, tipping his hat. "Sorry to bother you, Mrs. Silvers, but we wanted you to have a look at him."

The old woman quit rocking.

"Ever see him before?"

Seab said, "Be real sure, Mattie. You got to be sure."

She looked at the boy a long time before speaking; when she spoke her voice trembled. "He was in a blue suit. There on the road he wore a blue suit."

The boy shook his head.

"You're lying," Seab said.

"Mrs. Silvers . . ." said the deputy.

"He's lying," Seab said.

"Okay," the boy said suddenly. "She picked me up. But nothing happened. I swear to God nothing happened."

"Then, what'd you lie for?" the deputy said.

The boy blinked. "I was scared. I knew if I said I was in the truck . . . I knew you wouldn't believe me."

"Take him on out of here," Seab said.

"Tell them, lady . . ."

"You want me to rap you side the head?" the deputy said. "You'll get your chance to talk when the time comes. Is he the one, Mrs. Silvers?"

She was watching Seab. When he looked at her she shook her head slowly. "I don't know . . ." She hesitated. "He was there on the road and it commenced to rain. Things are so . . ."

"She asked me where I was going," the boy said. "I told her Memphis and she said she was going to Memphis, too. Then she started acting funny . . ."

"Get him out of here," Seab said.

"When she started acting funny I . . ."

Seab's fist shot out.

"Don't!" Mattie cried.

The boy fell against the deputy, his hand up to his mouth.

"Seab!" Mattie came up off the bed. "Don't hit him again! You hear me? Don't hit him again!"

Tears welled in the boy's eyes. He took the handkerchief the deputy handed him and pressed it to his mouth. When he pulled it away there was blood on it.

"Let him go," she said.

"Don't you see, mister . . . ?" The blood had run down onto the lapel of the boy's blue suit. "Don't you see it didn't happen that way . . . like you asked me about? Why, this lady's old enough . . ."

"Get him out of here before I kill him," Seab said.

"Kill me!" Mattie cried. "Kill me! He's just a boy. I'm old. Old enough . . ." Her voice broke, her fear and the cut-glass secret. There was a vision: the shattered pieces fell tinkling at the boy's feet; she stooped to pick them up.

"Whatever you folks want done . . ." the deputy said.

Seab stood clenching and unclenching his fists. He watched Mattie press her hands over her ears, watched her slump to the bed and lie still and small against the counterpane. "Listen to me, Mattie," he said. "You listening?"

She shook her head and rolled over in the bed, pushed the blanket away from her so that it fell off onto the floor.

"If it's him, say so, Mattie. That's all we wanted you to say."

The vision swept past Mattie, leaving her with long-forgotten memories, spotted like mirrors, reflecting here a face and there only the bare wall behind. The face in the memory mirror smiled at her and she returned the smile, but when she closed her eyes and opened them again there was only the bare wall. "Let him go," she said. She was looking out of the window and down the gravel road she could not see in the windy darkness. "Let him go."

The deputy was leading him out of the room. The gravel road and the highway beyond would lead him out of her life, on and on.

"You listening to me, Mattie?" Seab said.

She shook her head, her hands still pressed tight against her ears.

"Everything's all right, Mattie. He's gone. Everything's all right."

"Leave her alone," the old woman said. "Don't make her talk."

"You listening, Mattie?" Seab said again. "Because what happened up the Memphis highway don't matter to me. I don't want you to talk. I don't want you to talk and say what happened up the Memphis highway, because what happened don't matter to me."

Mattie closed her eyes. Outside she could hear rain beginning to fall. In the morning the darkness would be gone and no rain would fall. There would be bare fields and chinaberry trees and a canopy of cloud and sky, like a blue cup turned upside down over them. The face that for an instant smiled at her was gone, and she knew now it was a trick image, forever changing, like the tink-tink-tinkle of glass in a high wind.

Friday's
Child

Goddam, if it was me . . . or even Eleanor . . . I mean, you'd expect it of Eleanor. She'd done everything there was to do before she was twenty, and if she hadn't done it twice it was because there wasn't time to. Married Stanley Quin when she was eighteen, the same age as Billy. That was what her fight with Lewis was about, that and running up bills on his Memphis charge accounts. No daughter of his was going to run up a six-hundred-dollar bill giving ties and socks for Christmas. And when Eleanor talked right back to him, he slapped her, and she ran out of the house and got in that Buick and she's never set foot in that house again from that day to this. That is, until the wedding. And only because of Billy. That's what I mean . . . if it had been Eleanor or me, or anybody under the goddam sun but Billy. We had such hopes for him. Mama did. Eleanor did. All of us did.

Lewis was saying it too. The other night, before the wedding, we were talking and he said, "Billy . . ." You know, Lewis never lets you know how he feels; maybe he's afraid to. "Billy's the last . . ." The youngest and the last. There was me (I was thirty-two my last birthday), and then there was Eleanor, and then there was a ten-year gap before there was Billy. You know that saying. How does it go? *Monday's child is fair of face . . . Tuesday's child is full of grace . . . Wednesday's child is full of woe . . .* That's me. *Thursday's child has far to go . . .* That would be Eleanor. But Friday's child . . . Mama used to call Billy that. *Friday's child is loving and giving.* And Billy was.

I guess that's why Mama's not still with us today: she was too old to be having a baby, and it took a lot out of her. But, goddam, she loved that boy. And he loved her. He didn't leave the house that week before she died. Just sat there, and every so often she'd rouse and ask for a swallow of water, and Billy would bring her some water. I don't guess he's ever got over Mama's dying, sixteen and all, and never very close to Lewis. That's why I asked him if he didn't want to move in here with me. But he said he guessed he'd just stay there with Lewis. "I guess Daddy needs me," he said. Which was a lot of crap. I mean, Lewis never needed anybody. And Billy knew it. Maybe he'd heard that crap about me and my drinking problem. He knows how I like a drink. And it's not exactly a problem. I can quit any day I want to; it's just, to be frank, I don't want to.

Billy is the only one of us who calls Lewis Daddy. I don't know why. Once Billy asked me that, why it was we didn't

call Lewis Daddy or Papa or something, and I told him I
didn't know, and he said, "What did he do to you?"
And I laughed and said, "He never did a thing to me."
Which was the truth. It was not what Lewis did; it was
what he didn't do. He honored every check I ever wrote, I
will say that for him.

From the time Billy was twelve or so, he was always
close to me. Not *that* close: our ages were so different. But
I used to take him hunting. We'd go down on Beulah Lake,
and sometimes we wouldn't get back before night, and all
the way back in we'd talk. We could always talk. And
when this happened, I was the one he came to first. I guess
it wasn't easy. How're you going to tell a brother that much
older than you that you got a girl in trouble? Only Billy did
a pretty good job of it. "Bubba . . ." he said, and he looked
kind of sheepish, "you know I've been out a time or two
with Ida Margaret Cross . . ." To tell the truth, I didn't
know. "Anyway," he said, "it looks like . . . she's three
weeks overdue."

We kind of grinned at each other. You know how it is, as
if to say, *Boy, you been at it, haven't you?* Except Billy
wasn't the kind of boy who was out knocking up girls. Oh,
he liked the girls. But when Sonny Gibbs and Joe Wesley
and some of the others were out keeping that back seat
hot, Billy was on the track working out or working on some
biology project or other (once it was snakes) or out with
his Scout troop on some camporee. He was named Mr.
CHS his senior year, and the girls voted him the most
handsome, even after he broke his nose in that game with
Rolling Fork. It wasn't how handsome he was, or how smart.
And he was smart. He was just a nice boy. He could have
gone to any school he wanted to. And Lewis could have
fixed it so he got an appointment to the West Point Military
Academy. But Mama had her heart set on his going to

Ole Miss. Her daddy had gone to Ole Miss, and he was a doctor; I had flunked out of pre-med, and she wanted one of her boys to be a doctor. So that's where Billy went. That's where he went all last year, and I guess if he'd stayed for the summer term this wouldn't have happened. He came back here at the first of the summer and all of his crowd was gone—some of them married and some of them off at school—and that's how he started going with Ida Margaret Cross, I guess. Lewis let him have the car, and he was eighteen, and I guess one night it got so bad he couldn't help himself.

And when she was three weeks overdue he came to me. "We've been sweating it out," he said.

"Does she know it was you?" I said.

He looked at me like I was crazy or something. "Sure, she knows it was me," he said.

If it had been anybody but Billy I'd have told him what he could do: what we used to do. Get a signed statement. Get four or five of the boys to sign a statement that they had had it, too. But not Billy.

"I suppose the only thing," he said, "is for me to marry her."

"Ida Margaret Cross?" I said. It wasn't Ida Margaret. She's a right pretty little thing. It's the whole family—Luther Cross and all the rest of them.

"Well," he said, "I did it."

"Hell," I said, "that doesn't mean you have to marry her."

"She's a nice girl, Bubba," he said. That's Billy for you. "She's a real nice girl."

"But you wouldn't have married her."

He shook his head. "No," he said, "I don't suppose I would have married her."

But he did. He was hell-bent and determined to go

through with it, and nothing I said made any difference. Nothing Lewis said. Even Eleanor. "Baby," she said, "life's too short." And Lewis went to Luther Cross, told him he'd give her a rent house and five thousand dollars in cash and a paid-up education policy on the baby if she wouldn't go through with it. Luther would have taken it. I don't guess Ida Margaret would. By that time she was in love with Billy. Or, at least, she thought she was. After all, Billy was quite a catch, good-looking, even with a broken nose, Mr. CHS and all. And Billy was upset when he heard what Lewis had done, because he figured Ida Margaret would figure *he* sent him. She didn't, of course. She knew Billy. I tell you, he was . . . well, he was a kind of little god to us . . . what we wanted to be ourselves and never had been and never would be. Like Eleanor. Married at eighteen and divorced and married again at twenty-one to a goddam alcoholic. "Don't call Jim an alcoholic," she said, like who am I to call him one, and I said, "Listen, sweetie, I may have a problem but I can quit any day I want to."

"Tell another one," she said.

And I said, "Okay, okay, I'm a two-time loser myself." First it was Edith, you know, and then this Memphis girl. Maybe I'm hard to get along with. But, goddam, I admit it.

The trouble with Eleanor . . . the trouble with me too . . . is we never gave a damn. We never wondered about whether what we did mattered, whether it mattered if we got drunk and turned over a car on the road to Rolling Fork or whether Lewis would bail us out if we got ourselves in jail. Which he had to once. A bunch of us took over this nigger dance hall. Oh, just for a lark, you know. And the sheriff picked us up, and Lewis said he should have let us spend the night in jail, only he didn't, of course.

Mama wouldn't have let him. "Now, Bubba . . ." she said. I can hear her now. "What you want to do *that* for?"

Maybe because there was nothing else to do. Maybe because when you're eighteen and it's a summer night this place gets next to you. The smoke from those nigger cabins and that smell from the river: that river goes somewhere, and you want to follow it. Maybe it was the same with Billy. Eighteen and driving around in that Pontiac with the radio going and the tires slapping the highway, and that girl there on the seat by him. That ache. Goddam, that ache.

The Crosses wanted to make it a big wedding, in the church and everything, but Lewis said no. Just a quiet wedding at home, he said. Not even at the bride's home, because the bride didn't have much home—oh, nothing to be ashamed of, but nothing to brag about either. So Lewis offered the big house. And he brought a woman decorator down from Memphis to sprucen up the place. He never scrimped where Billy was concerned. Billy didn't want all that. He would just as soon have been married in the preacher's study, and I think I would agree with him.

So Lewis asked me to get in touch with Eleanor, and I did, and at first she said she wouldn't come. She had sworn she'd never go back in that house. You know she never did, not even when she came for Mama's funeral. The funeral was held from the church, which made it, for her at least, goddam convenient. All during Mama's lifetime she'd call Mama from Memphis and say, "I'm coming home. I'll meet you at Bolton's Drug Store at such and such a time." And Mama and Billy would go down to Bolton's Drug Store and sit there at one of those tables in the back, and pretty soon Eleanor would come driving up. And they'd sit and talk. Maybe Mama would take Eleanor up the street and buy her a box of hose or a pretty pin, some little something such as that, and then Eleanor would kiss them both good-by and she was off again to Memphis. Every time Mama would say, "Sister, when are you coming home?" And Sister would say, "Mama, you know I'm not going back there as long as *he's* alive." I guess that hurt Mama. Poor Mama. Me and Eleanor both. So she put all of her hopes in Billy.

He was sixteen when Mama died, and he never did cry. Not that day, and he was there; not even at the funeral. I remember thinking how funny that was. One night, I guess it must have been a week or two afterward, Billy didn't get home for supper and Lewis got worried and sent me up to the school to look for him. I found him on the track. The moon was out and Billy was just running. Not fast. Just around the track, and around again, and I called his name, and when he came around again, caught him by the arm, and I said, "What you trying to do, Billy?"

Then he started to cry. Goddam, I thought he wasn't going to stop. A big boy like that. Just crying his heart out. I didn't say anything. I sat there on the bleachers by him, looking out across that field, and after a while he quit sniffing and he wiped his nose on his arm and said, "How old was Mama when you were born?"

"Oh," I said, and I thought, that's a goddam funny question, "in her twenties." And I figured. "Twenty-six, I guess." Then I knew what he meant. To him she was an old woman. She had always been an old woman.

"I miss her," he said.

"Yeah," I said, "so do I."

And he sat there a while, and then he said, "How much longer is it going to take?"

How much longer? I thought. "Oh," I said, "the worst is over." But it wasn't, and I knew it, and he knew it too, I guess.

That was all he ever said. I mean, about Mama. Until that night he came to me. Ida Margaret was three weeks overdue and he was going to marry her, and nothing I could say made any difference. "You know what this means?" I said. "You won't go back to school. . . ."

And he said, "What makes you say that?"

"Because you won't," I said.

He said he would, because that's what Mama wanted, and I said I hoped he meant it. But five . . . six years . . . however long it takes . . . that's a hell of a long time. And that's not the point, is it—whether Billy goes back to school or not, or ever finishes? Because what happened . . . well, it's happened before. It'll happen again. But, goddam, not to Billy.

The wedding was bigger than Lewis intended. The Crosses had invited a whole lot of their relatives, and Ida Margaret's three sisters were bridesmaids, and Luther gave the bride away. For free, when he could have kept her for a rent house and five thousand dollars in cash and an education policy. When the preacher said, "Who gives this woman?" I bet you Luther thought of it.

Some of Billy's friends gave him a stag party down at the hotel the night before the wedding. There was a whole lot of drinking. Billy did a little himself, and Sonny Gibbs presented him with a big box which was stuffed with wads of paper, and way down at the bottom there was a green prescription bottle filled with screws. Sonny had written on it: ONE EVERY FOUR HOURS, FOR RELIEF. And Billy laughed at that. We all did, though considering the circumstances I guess it wasn't so funny. When it was over, I drove Billy by the house and I was feeling pretty good myself and we sat there for a minute or two before he got out, the way we used to. We'd come in from hunting or from a day down on the lake and we'd sit there and talk: how many birds we killed or how many fish we caught, nothing very world-shaking, just something such as that. And I thought: this is the last time; we won't sit here any more like this. "Old Billy boy," I said, "so you're really going to do it?"

"Yeah, I think I will," he said, and he kind of grinned.

"Well, it's never too late, you know . . ." I said it for a joke. And I laughed. But I guess Billy knew I meant it.

After the wedding the next day there was a reception, and the last I saw of Billy he and Ida Margaret were trying to get away without the others seeing them. Lewis had given them a new convertible, and I had parked it on the road outside of town, and I took them out to it. But Sonny Gibbs was close behind. "If anybody needs to get in touch with us," Billy hollered, and he waved, "we'll be at the Buena Vista."

"Have a good time," I said, and I saw he got the message.

When I got back to the house, Lewis and Eleanor were at it again. He had asked her if she didn't want to spend the night at home, and she was telling him why she wouldn't. And not being too nice about it, either.

"Well, it's been a long time . . ." he said. He was drinking, too, and feeling sentimental.

"Well, I'll be back," she said, "for Billy's second wedding."

That made Lewis mad. "I've been as nice as I know how," he said. "As far as I'm concerned . . ."

"What?" she said, just baiting him. "What?"

"You can get the hell out of here . . ."

Eleanor laughed. "I will," she said, "when I get good and ready."

For a long time after Lewis had gone upstairs to bed we sat there on the steps. We had brought our drinks with us. "Bubba . . . poor Bubba," she said. "You're acting like Billy's dead."

"Yeah," I said. I could still hear Luther Cross's wife saying,

What a handsome couple, what a handsome couple, and I kept thinking of Billy boy off there in the Buena Vista Hotel with that prescription bottle filled with screws and those pajamas Sonny and Joe had tied together so he couldn't get them on and that pregnant bride there in the bed with him. Oh, Billy boy, I thought.

"Cheer up," Eleanor said.

And Billy running. I thought of that too. Around and around the track, there in the moonlight. *How much longer is it going to take?* he said. And I could have told him. But you have to learn that for yourself. "Yeah," I said, "cheer up. This is a goddam wedding, not a funeral."

Four
Minutes
to the
Bridge

In a minute, Miss Lottie thought, I'll go. But she was slow getting dressed. She had to look for her things, and when she found them she discovered that the sash was gone from the dress. She must have taken it off after the party at Angelina's house. Angelina had given a party and John Scott Underwood was there and John Scott said . . . No, she thought, I can't remember what he said. But something nice. So she took the sash from one of the other dresses, and got out the hat that her mother had always liked, and she went to look at herself. I want to look my best, she thought. I haven't seen John Scott in . . . how long? And this thing, this favor she was going to ask . . . Dear God, she thought, what is the world coming to?

Even as she stood looking in the mirror, the sounds of progress were around her. The bulldozers were plowing the earth on both sides of her house. In the ten blocks straight ahead of her, workmen were laying the concrete foundation for the new expressway to the bridge. And from her back window, as far as she could see, for the width of a block there was not a house or tree. Judge Ramsey's house—she had sat on that gallery a hundred afternoons. And the Fowler house. They had cut it half in two. She had watched them carry it down the street on the back of a truck, like a great dead thing, and as it passed, the half of it, she had wondered what Angelina Fowler would have said. That tongue! Oh, she would have liked to know what Angelina would have said. Or Effie Bruce. The Bruce house had passed too. She had run out on her gallery and hollered to a Negro boy, "You there, boy."

The Negro turned and looked at her.

"That house . . . is that Miss Effie Bruce's house?"

The Negro nodded his head.

They don't say yessum any more, she thought.

They had taken the Bruce house, the other houses in those twenty blocks, but they would not take hers. This house—it was the house her grandfather built. During her mother's lifetime she had kept it as it was; later she had found it necessary to rent the other side of it. And so she had brought in carpenters and they had sealed the doors and papered over them. Poor Mama, she thought, those strangers in her rooms. And she moved her mother's furniture. Now the renters were gone—scared off by the city's threats.

But they don't scare me, Miss Lottie thought. For three months she had stayed at home. There was no need to go;

Mr. Michelli delivered her groceries. Oh, she had gone as far as the walk. And she had seen them watching her, the people who passed in their cars. She knew what they thought: she was out of her head. She had turned down the money offered her. Sixteen thousand dollars. As if they could put a price on it. "No," she said.

They wanted to be fair, they said. They would move her house. They would find another lot for her. If it was a matter of money . . .

It was not. They sent the Mayor to call on her.

"I'm J. B. Hobbs," the Mayor said.

"I knew your father," Miss Lottie said, and she started to add, "though I never had much use for him."

The Mayor spoke at length of the city's growth, the traffic count, and the need for the new expressway route. "Why, Miss Sykes," he said, with the fervor of a man who was offering her his life, "this expressway will save four minutes to the bridge."

Miss Lottie looked at him. "Mr. Hobbs," she said, and she tried to be polite, "let me make myself perfectly clear. I will have no part of this plot to take my property."

"Miss Sykes . . ." he said.

"No," she said.

"I'm sure some settlement . . ."

"There will be," she said, "no settlement."

And so there was none. They filed a suit. They threatened her. They would expropriate her property. At last, she was summoned to appear in court; when the summons came, she did not answer it. The court ruled. She was awarded three thousand dollars more than the sum they had offered her. She was given ninety days to vacate the property. The check came by registered mail. She returned it. And when the ninety days was up, she ignored their notices.

But she stayed close to the house, going only now and

then as far as the walk, or sitting on her gallery, watching the people pass. Who are these people? she wondered. Where were they when Elias Sykes came down the river on a flatboat and settled the ground on which the Statehouse stands? Why should she give up her house to save them four minutes to the bridge? And what was on the other side? More highway. That was the trouble nowadays. People moved. Nobody stayed where they were. They spent their lives moving. They had no homes. Cars, but no homes. She had been born in this house, she had slept in it every night of her life, and, God willing, she would die in it. Change! Even that wall . . . moving her mother's furniture. There was a feeling she had, not only for the house itself but for the people she loved who had lived in it. That was why, when the carpenters came, she had left the front door as it was. The door was on the other side. On the side she kept for herself there were windows opening on the gallery. They were large windows; they ran from close to the ceiling down to the floor. By lifting the glass, or in summer the screen, she could step out on the gallery.

She knew what people said: *Lottie Sykes is climbing in and out of her windows.* She saw it in the Mayor's face, that day he came to call on her, though he never mentioned it.

Jed Rogers did. "Lottie . . ." he said. He had knocked at the door. She had called him to the window screen.

"Jed Rogers . . ." she said. He was a cousin of hers. Before her mother died, the families had visited. "I declare . . ."

"It's been a long time."

"It has," she said. Now where did I see him last? she thought. At somebody's funeral. "Come in." And she lifted the screen.

He laughed. "What's this, you letting me in through the window?"

"Oh," she said, "I had renters. I let them have the other side."

"You let them have your door?"

She nodded.

"And you kept your windows." He smiled.

"Sit down," she said. He sat down. She sat on the sofa next to him. "How've you been?"

"Oh, pretty good," he said, "considering."

"And Hattie? How's Hattie?"

He looked at her for a moment. "You know, Lottie," he said, "Hattie . . ." He laughed again. "I declare, it's good to see you," he said. "How've you been?"

"Oh," she said, "I'd be all right if they'd just leave me alone. They've been after me to sell my property."

"That's what I hear," he said.

"You don't know," she said.

"And I've been meaning to come. I don't get out much any more. I tried calling you. They said you didn't have a phone."

"After Mama died," she said, "I had the phone disconnected."

"I thought . . ."

"Look out there," she said. "All those houses . . . I tell you, it makes you sad."

"Lottie . . ."

She looked at him.

"The reason I came . . ." He cleared his throat. "I have a little piece of property out here next to the Weller place. You know the Weller place. It's not the best property, but there's some shade trees on it. And you could put this house on it."

The anger filled her throat. "No," she said.

"I don't mean sell it," he said. "Why, it's not worth that much. I mean, if you want it you can have it."

"Well, that's mighty nice of you," she said, "but you see . . ." She got up and she felt the ache in her. "I was born in this house. But it's not just this house . . ."

"Lottie . . ."

She thought of the bridge, and of that dream she had had. She was standing on the bridge, there below the silver girders, and the wind was in her hair, and then she was falling . . . falling. . . .

"How long did they give you?" he said.

"Give me?"

"To vacate the property."

"Oh," she said. "Ninety days."

"When was that?"

"It's up," she said. "It's been up. They keep sending me notices."

"Where will you go? When they move this house . . ."

"They'll never move this house," she said.

"Lottie . . ." He smiled at her. "You can't fight the law, Lottie."

"Whose law?" Again the anger filled her throat. First the lawyers, then the Mayor, now Jed Rogers telling her. "Whose law?"

"Lottie . . ." He spoke slowly. "I've been knowing you all my life; why, my mama and your mama were cousins. I came here as a friend, Lottie. Only as a friend."

She turned away from him.

"Do you think I'd come here . . . ?" For a moment he sat there. Then slowly, as if he expected her to say, "No, don't go," he got up.

She held out her hand to him.

There was some secret sorrow in his face. "Good-by, Lottie," he said.

"Good-by," she said. She saw him to the gallery.

She had gone back in the house when suddenly, out of her head, something came to her. *I asked about Hattie,* she thought, *and Hattie's dead.* "Jed Rogers . . ." She ran to the window. He was gone. But across the street two men were watching her.

The same two men. Early this morning she had caught them on her property. She had heard a noise in the front, the sound of a voice, and had gone to check on it. A man was in her flower bed. When she reached the gallery she saw that there were two of them. "Get out of this yard," she said.

They did not seem to notice her.

"What you got?" one said.

"Thirty-eight," the other said.

"Get away from this house!" she cried.

The men turned and walked off in the direction of the bulldozer that was plowing the earth on the side to the south of her.

The nerve, she thought. And she made her way through the house to get a swallow of the brandy she kept in her armoire for times such as this when her hands trembled and her heart pounded and her knees seemed about to give way under her. By the time she found the brandy her heart was beating right again. But the apprehension hung to her. She lay down on the bed, her eyes closed, trying to tell herself it was nothing, they had gone, they would not be coming back. She did not believe it. For the first time in a very long time she felt alone. She needed someone. But who? She thought of her father. She wondered how her father would have handled this. Or her mother. *If Mama was here . . . ,* she thought.

Then she heard them. She went out on the gallery. They were measuring the other way.

"Forty-four."

She hurried back into the house, back into her room, closed the hall door after her. Dear God, she thought, who? In all this world, who? And there in the room it came to her. *John Scott.* John Scott Underwood. They had grown up together. He had once proposed to her. And there at the party at Angelina's house . . . he was a young lawyer then. Later, like so many others she had known, he made his name in politics—first as judge, and then as governor. John Scott. Who could help her but the Governor? And John Scott would.

She was slow getting dressed. She had to look for her things, and when she found them she discovered that the sash was gone from the dress. So she took the sash from one of the other dresses, and got out the hat that her mother had always liked, and then, giving herself a last look, went out through the window, careful to fold the shutters behind. She walked out to the edge of the gallery. There was no one in sight, only the men on the bulldozers, and they were not watching her. With quick steps she hurried down the walk and across the narrow strip of grass to the street. A car approached. She waved her hand. It stopped in front of her.

"Young man," she said, one hand on her hat to keep the wind from taking it, "I wonder if you'd be so kind as to let me ride with you?"

"Why, yes mam," he said. And he got out and opened the door for her. They all did. All the young men opened the door for her.

"I'm going to the Statehouse," she said. "If it's out of your way . . ."

"I go right by there," he said.

"Well, I wouldn't want to put you out of your way . . ."

"You're Miss Lottie Sykes, aren't you?"

"Yes," she said, and it pleased her that he knew. "You knew my family?"

"No," he said, and smiled, "but I've been reading about you in the papers."

"In the papers?" she said.

"They've taken your property . . ."

"Yes . . ." She wondered what the papers said. "They've been after me to sell my property."

He drove on, past the blocks that had been leveled to make room for the new expressway to the bridge.

"Do I know you?" Miss Lottie said.

The young man smiled. "I don't think so. I'm Dave Levy."

Jews, she thought. "No," she said, "I don't know your family."

"My mother was an Abraham."

"Oh, yes," she said. "Mr. Abraham runs the ready-to-wear . . ."

"That was my grandfather."

Louis Abraham. He had sold her this dress. Now she remembered. This very dress. *Little lady* . . . , he said. He had a funny way of talking. *This dress is very stylish.* And her mother said, *Yes, Sister, it does look good on you.*

"His store was there," the young man said.

Miss Lottie looked. She tried to remember where his store had been, at what end of that parking lot. And she saw the people on the street: the men in shirt sleeves and the women in house dresses. Downtown in house dresses! No one that she recognized. They were near the Statehouse now. She saw the white columns and the golden dome and she remembered why she had come and what she would say. *John Scott* . . . And she said, "John Scott," aloud, and the young man looked at her. She smiled. "I'm going to see the Governor."

"I can let you out at the side," he said.

"No," she said. "I can get out here. This will be fine."

He pulled over and stopped.

"Don't get out," she said, but he was already out. He opened the door for her. "Well, I'm much obliged to you," she said, "Mr. . . ."

"Levy."

"Levy." Yes, she thought, you're Louis Abraham's grandson. I can see it now, the eyes.

"It was my pleasure," he said.

Such a nice young man, she thought. And so polite. For a moment she stood there. The wind whipped the brim of her hat. "You know what they told me?" she said. "They told me they wanted my property and I asked them why, and you know what they said?"

The young man looked at her.

"It would save four minutes to the bridge."

"Four minutes," he said, and laughed. And still he looked at her.

But he doesn't understand, she thought. And who does? Who, in all this world, does? And she turned, her back now to him, and hurried toward the Statehouse steps.

When she stood under that great dome, she remembered standing there before. She was a child and her father had taken her to see the Governor. She could not even remember now what governor it was, or which way they had gone, which office was the Governor's. But she asked, and a stranger took her there, led her up the stairs and down the hall to a room with heavy double doors on which was written GOVERNOR. There was a woman at a desk. The walls were dark. The floor was carpeted. "Good morning," the woman said. "Is there something I can do for you?"

Miss Lottie caught her breath. "I've come to see the Governor."

"You have an appointment?"

"No, but . . ."

"Oh, I'm sorry," the woman said, "but I'm afraid you'll have to have an appointment to see the Governor."

Miss Lottie stood there. She looked at the woman and the woman looked at her. "If you tell him Lottie Sykes . . ."

The woman smiled, as if she remembered the name. "Miss Sykes, I'm sure the Governor would be happy to see you another time."

"I have to see him now," she said. She felt the ache in her.

"Well, I'm afraid," the woman said, "that won't be possible. You see, the Governor is in conference. He'll be in conference all morning. Perhaps if you came back . . ."

"Then I'll wait," Miss Lottie said. And she sat down suddenly. John Scott . . . she thought. Why, we grew up together. But it's been a long time. I wonder if he'll know me. I wonder if I'll have to say, *John Scott . . . John Scott, this is Lottie. . . .*

In a little while the woman said, "Miss Sykes," and her voice was friendlier, "perhaps if you told me what it was you wanted to see the Governor about . . ."

Miss Lottie cocked her head. "The Governor," she said, "is an old old friend of mine."

"Well, as I say . . ." The woman smiled. "You can wait if you like . . . perhaps he can see you later . . . but at the moment he's in conference."

And so Miss Lottie waited. She had arrived at half past eight. At ten the Governor was still in conference. At ten fifteen a man arrived she did not know and asked to see the Governor. "Come right this way," the woman said. "He's been expecting you."

John Scott . . . Miss Lottie thought. When I tell him how they've treated me . . . and not only this woman. The others, too. I mean, beginning to end. Oh, she thought,

those letters, those ugly letters . . . trying to get me to sell
my property. And those lawyers, and the Mayor himself . . .
coming there the way they did. And then this other . . .
this morning, there in the yard . . . She thought of the men,
and the fear came back to her. Dear God, she thought, I
hope John Scott remembers me.

"Miss Sykes . . ."

It was the woman. Miss Lottie looked at her.

"I spoke to the Governor a moment ago. He says if you'll
wait he'll try to see you a little after twelve. He's sorry to
have kept you waiting."

"After twelve?" Miss Lottie frowned. The thought of it
angered her. But her anger quickly cooled. John Scott
would talk to her at twelve. He was sorry to have kept her
waiting. She would say, *John Scott* . . . No, *Governor* . . .
He would like that. *Governor, I'll bet you don't know who
this is.* And he would say, *Lottie* . . . *Lottie Sykes. Why, of
course, I do.*

Miss Lottie waited. An hour passed. A half hour. She
heard a clock strike twelve. At a quarter after she was on
her way to see the Governor. The woman led her into
another room and across the polished floors she remembered as a child and down another hall to the room with
the great white door. The woman opened it.

Miss Lottie walked into the room. The light from the
windows blinded her. Then she made out the figure of a
man behind a desk. He was getting up. He was coming
toward her. "Governor . . ." The pulse was pounding in
her throat.

"Miss Sykes . . ."

The face loomed before her. It was a face that she had
never seen. Dear God, she thought. For an instant she
started to run.

"I'm sorry you had to wait, Miss Sykes . . ."

"John Scott . . ." she said. "John Scott Underwood."

The face before her turned away.

"I came to see the Governor . . ."

There was a silence.

Then he spoke. "Governor Underwood?"

"Yes," she said.

"Miss Sykes . . ." He turned and looked at her. "Miss Sykes, Governor Underwood has been dead . . . Governor Underwood died in 1948, I think it was."

"No," Miss Lottie said. But even as she did, she remembered John Scott, and she remembered that someone had said to her, long ago, *John Scott Underwood is dead.* "Dear God!" she cried.

"Miss Sykes . . ."

She closed her eyes.

"Miss Sykes, I'm Governor Harper . . ."

Governor Harper? she thought. I don't remember a Governor Harper. She opened her eyes. She looked at him. "Are you Nola Harper's son?"

He shook his head.

He's not Nola Harper's son, she thought. I don't know him. He doesn't know me.

"Is there something I can do?" he said.

"No," she said. "I want to go home."

"Well, I'll have my chauffeur drive you. Where do you live?"

She did not answer him.

"Miss Sykes . . ."

"Beyond Judge Ramsey's," she said.

He took her by the arm and walked beside her out into the hall and down the stairs and out to where the car was waiting. A hearse, Miss Lottie thought. But it was not a hearse. There was a Negro driver and he was dressed in black, and he opened the door for her.

For a moment she hesitated.

"Good-by, Miss Sykes," the Governor said.

Still she stood there.

He smiled. "Governor Underwood . . . you knew Governor Underwood?"

She nodded.

"He was a fine gentleman."

Yes, she thought, he was a fine gentleman.

"Take Miss Sykes home," the Governor said.

She got in and the Negro got in front and then the car began to move. It rolled down the drive past the Statehouse steps and out into the street, and the Negro turned and spoke to her. "The Governor said you'd show me . . ."

"Beyond Judge Ramsey's," she said. And then she thought, No, there's nothing there. There's no house there. And she said, "Out Government."

The car moved on. She watched the blocks of empty ground. She even counted them. In the distance, like some terror in a dream, she saw the bridge. Its silver girders caught the sun. And as she drew near she saw her own house, the house where she was born. The men were moving it.

Night
Watch

When Toler came on duty a little before ten, Mr. Joe was already there. He generally got down to the city hall right at about nine o'clock, unless the fights were on or Ella wanted him to keep the grandbabies while she and Earl went to the picture show. Mr. Joe didn't mind; those babies were his life. But he liked to get there early, so he and Wade could talk a while. When Toler came on, he was sitting there in the chair, his hat back on his head and his feet up on the desk. "Looks like it's going to be a bad night," he said. Toler said, "Yeah." A rain had started to fall, and the streets were wet. "Good for the crops," Mr. Joe said.

"Well, you boys are here, I think I'll turn in," Wade said.

Wade worked the two to ten, the shift Mr. Joe worked until he reached sixty and Tom McLean moved him over to the night side. There wasn't much to do at night, after midnight anyway, except keep strange niggers off the street and see that the lights stayed on in the back of those stores. If one of those lights went out, Mr. Joe was over there. He never used his gun, but he never had to. The niggers were scared of him. "How many more days?" Wade said.

"Oh, eight or nine," Mr. Joe said, like it didn't make any difference.

But it does, Toler thought. He wondered if the old man blamed him, for taking his place and all. Well, if it wasn't me . . . , he thought. Anyway, if he was going to blame somebody, it ought to be Mr. Tom. And maybe he did. He didn't say much, but Toler had a pretty good idea how he felt. Nine more days and he'd be off the payroll, with nothing to do but sit around home, not even his home, his daughter's, minding his grandbabies, or most likely sitting around down here, because he had spent most of his life here in this two-by-four building under the water tank.

As a matter of fact, Mr. Joe was thinking about Tom McLean tonight. He thought about him more and more, how he had broken Tom in when Tom was no older than this boy was now. They were together that day Al Faducci came running out of the pool hall and shot two niggers on the street, and they had to go up to Shelby after him. And when Peller Wade, Wade here's brother, tried to beat the noon train to the crossing, and didn't, they helped to put him in the ambulance. And they had hunted together over on Beulah Lake. When Tom's boy drowned, on one of those hunting trips, it was Joe who fished him out, and came close to drowning doing it. Maybe Tom had forgotten all that. *You know I'd keep you on if I could,* Tom said. *Goddam, you been here thirty years. Close to, anyway. But the law's the law.* That didn't satisfy Joe. Bringing in this boy who wouldn't know what to do if a drunk nigger come at him, except maybe kill him. Oh, he thought, these young ones got a lot to learn.

And Toler thought: It'll kill him. He'll come down here at night and sit and talk to Wade and me, and he won't last a year.

"Before I get away," Wade said, "Tom said keep an eye out for any carloads of niggers coming through. They run a carload of 'em in yesterday over in Sunflower County."

"What for?" Toler said.

Mr. Joe smiled. "Oh," he said, "general principles."

"Black sonsabitches," Wade said. "Well," he said, "I'm going to turn it over to you. If you have any trouble . . ."

No, Mr. Joe thought, I got nine more days and I don't want any trouble. He watched Wade, standing there at the door, waiting for the rain to slack, and he thought: He's not going to set any crosses tonight; it's too wet. Once he had smelled the kerosene on Wade's clothes, but he never mentioned it. And he kept telling himself: That's as far as he'd go. Because he liked Wade, and why would a man like that . . . ? Then the rain slacked, and he saw Wade duck his head and make a run for it.

"You ready?" Toler said.

Mr. Joe got up and got his flashlight off the cabinet and checked his forty-five and said, "You better check yours." So Toler checked his. He had already, but he didn't want Mr. Joe to think he was impudent. "I guess I'll drive tonight," he said. Every night he said that, and every night Mr. Joe said, "All right, you drive tonight," as if it was all right with him. Tom McLean had told him he didn't want him to drive because he couldn't see as good as he used to.

"Let's drive up to Ellzey's," Mr. Joe said. Ellzey ran a service station up on the highway. That was the first place

Mr. Joe went, because Ellzey closed at ten thirty and Mr. Joe wanted to get him some free cigarettes.

"Seen any niggers in out-of-state cars tonight?" Mr. Joe said.

"No, sir," Ellzey said. "Traffic's been mighty slow. The rain, I guess."

"Wade says they run in a carload yesterday over in Sunflower County."

"That's what I saw in the paper," Ellzey said. "You expecting trouble?"

Mr. Joe smiled. "Not me," he said. "I guess those niggers are. And when you go out and look for trouble, you generally find it. You know Toler here, don't you?"

"Sure," Ellzey said.

"He's taking my place the first of the month." The old man had told him that a half a dozen times.

It's on his mind, Toler thought.

"What you hear from Wayne?" Ellzey's boy was in the Army.

"Mr. Joe," Ellzey said, "his mother and me got a letter the other day. He's been sent out in Texas. Camp Somethinorother."

"That's good," Mr. Joe said. He wasn't even listening. "Toler here was in the Army."

"Yeah?" Ellzey said.

"Just got out. Wasn't it in April?"

Toler nodded.

"Since then got him a wife. How long's it been?"

"A couple of months," Toler said.

"A couple of months." Mr. Joe laughed. "I expect it's hard to be gone from home at night when you been married a couple of months."

Toler grinned. "Yeah, it's pretty hard," he said. They always want to know, he thought: I guess, comparing.

After they left Ellzey's they drove around the town. It was still raining. There was a car with a flat tire on the road behind the school, and Toler put on his raincoat and got out and helped the boy to fix it. "You from here?" he said. "No, sir," the boy said, "from over near Gunnison." There was a girl in the car, and when Toler shined the light inside to look for the jack he caught a glimpse of her. He thought of Wilda, back there in the bed asleep, and he thought: First thing I'm going to do when I get home in the morning, if I'm not too tired, is knock me off a piece.

They stopped by the café to get a cup of coffee and for Mr. Joe to pay for his supper the night before, and then they went over to the telephone office. Mr. Joe always checked by the telephone office, to see if there had been any calls for him, but mainly to talk to Miss Maud, who had been the night operator since before he came to Laurason.

"Anything going on, Miss Maud?"

"Not a thing," she said. She was sitting at the switchboard making an afghan. "Mighty quiet. And that," she said, "is the way I like it."

"You know Toler here, don't you?"

"Why, sure," Miss Maud said. "How're you, Mr. Toler? I do know something," she said. "There's been some niggers in Chicago calling some niggers over in Shelby, and the calls have been coming through here."

"Humh," Mr. Joe said. "What you guess those niggers are up to?"

"Well, I don't know . . ." she said, and just then the switchboard buzzed and she plugged in a cord and answered, "Number, please?" It was long distance. "For Huntley Dunn," she said. "That woman up in Memphis. She gets drunk and every night about this time puts in a call to him. . . ."

"This late?" Mr. Joe said.

"This late," she said. "Hello . . . is this the Memphis operator?"

"Miss Maud . . ."

Miss Maud didn't hear him. She was busy trying to put the call through.

"We're going to mosey on," Mr. Joe said. "There's supposed to be some carloads of niggers . . ."

"Niggers?" she said. And then she said, "Excuse it, Operator." They had heard her in Memphis.

"Nothing to worry about," said Mr. Joe.

"Well, lock the door good. . . . Hello, Operator . . ." Miss Maud waved.

When they came down out of the telephone office, the rain had stopped. By then it was after twelve o'clock and the streets were deserted. "You want me to pull over there?" Toler said. "Yeah," Mr. Joe said. He put his hand to his stomach. That pain again. What is it? he thought. And the boy saw him and said, "You feeling all right?"

"Yeah," he said. "Pull on over there like I showed you." It was across the street from the picture show, where he could watch the whole street, the stores, and the lights in the back of them. If one went out, he knew it. And where he could watch the traffic passing through. It had to turn down this street and it had to slow the block before to go around the monument, and Mr. Joe, though he couldn't see to drive, could spot an out-of-state car at fifty yards. At least, he said so.

"What time is it?" he said.

"Twenty after twelve," Toler said.

"This would be about the time they'd come through."

"This time of night?"

"Oh," Mr. Joe said, "you don't know a nigger. A nigger'll try to cause you all the trouble he can."

No, Toler thought, I don't know a nigger. The only nigger he knew was a cook named Bea, and sometimes, when he was a boy, those summers, Bea would take him home with her. She'd feed him pie. And she'd get out those pictures, those funny brown pictures, because he asked her to. Why would a nigger want to have his picture taken? He remembered thinking that, as if that was something no nigger did. But the nigger he knew died, swelled up with dropsy and had to be tapped, and never came again to cook for them. His mother cried. He remembered that. *Beatrice,* she said, *loved you.* And whenever Toler remembered, he smelled that house. The smell came back to him.

"You know what to do, don't you?" Mr. Joe said.

Toler looked at him.

"If you see one coming through . . ."

"Get in behind him?"

"As soon as you see," Mr. Joe said. "It takes practice. You got to size it up all at once. And you don't look for the same things you used to. You used to look for an old Ford or a Chevy with a squirrel tail on the radiator cap. Or big hubcaps. Niggers used to like big hubcaps. It's the big cars now. You won't find any of those niggers from Chicago in a Ford. You look for a Cadillac—or maybe a Buick. But you got to be careful." Mr. Joe laughed. "One time—oh, it was a couple of years back—Wade caught a glimpse of this big car barreling ass down the street, and it looked like to him it was just full of niggers. So he took out behind it and he turned the siren on and he got 'em to pull over just before they left the city limits. *What you niggers think you're doing?* he said. Well . . ." Mr. Joe laughed again. "It wasn't niggers at all. It was Governor Ross Barnett, headed for Memphis."

"That was Wade?" Toler said.

"Yeah," Mr. Joe said, "that was Wade." That Wade, he

thought. His daddy never was that way. Or his granddaddy, old Judge Wade. The old judge had a nigger boy to drive him, and when he got old and had those strokes that nigger took care of him, still took him for rides sometimes, sitting up there in the back seat with his head propped on a pillow, and when they stopped at the post office, everybody saying, *Evening, Judge Wade. How you feeling, Judge Wade?* and him never answering. Even the niggers. All the niggers respected him. But Wade . . . his brothers, too. It must have been that Redmon blood: their mother was a Redmon. Mr. Joe remembered how his Aunt Lily Baxter used to ask that. *Now,* she'd say, and you knew it was very important, *who was your mother?* And if your mother was a Baxter or a Dunn, or even a Wade, it was all right, but if she was a Redmon his Aunt Lily would just say, *Oh.* That was all. *Oh.* "You were in the Army," Mr. Joe said. "I guess there was plenty of niggers in the Army."

"Yeah," Toler said.

"They ever give you any trouble?"

"No," he said. And then he remembered the nigger sergeant. "Well, yeah," he said. "Up at Camp Lee there was a nigger sergeant, and he was a bastard. Ate everybody's ass out. Boys from the South especially. So some of us got together and one weekend when we caught that nigger sergeant off the base . . ." Toler smiled. "We messed him up pretty bad. Busted his nose. Broke a couple of his ribs. So the Army got him out of there."

"Oh, you give a nigger an inch . . ." Mr. Joe said. And he thought: I bet those white boys stomped that nigger good. Beat the whey out of him. White boys nowadays are mean. I wouldn't have wanted to see it.

"If some do come through," Toler said, "and you get in behind 'em and bring 'em in, what you charge 'em with?"

"Speeding," said Mr. Joe. "If they try to give you any

trouble, resisting arrest. If they give you too much trouble
. . ." He thought of Wade. "Rap one side the head. But not
with your fist," he said. "You know how hard a nigger's
head is. You'll break your fist. The butt of your gun. Or a
brick. I used to carry me a brick."

I bet you used it, Toler thought. He remembered the
night the boys jumped that nigger sergeant, and how when
they got him down they started to kick him, and he tried
to kick him and couldn't. But this old man, he thought, this
old man has seen some things. He'd kick a nigger as soon
as look at him. And he thought: What is it? What makes a
man like that, who could go and sit with his grandbabies,
and who would give you the shirt off his back if he thought
you needed it?

"Oh," Mr. Joe said, "things have changed since I was a
boy. I grew up out here on the Baxter place. Had niggers
to play with when I was a boy. Got a little nigger stuff
too. . . ." He laughed. "You know what they say: a Southern boy's not a Southern boy until he's had him a little
nigger stuff. I don't know about you . . ."

Well, then, I guess, Toler thought, I'm not a Southerner.

"No," Mr. Joe said, "things have changed. I remember one
time, oh, I guess it must have been when I was twelve or
so, back before the First World's War. My daddy run a
commissary. And all the niggers used to buy there. Well, he
started missing things. First it was a cheese. One of those
big round cheeses. And then some smoked sausage, and
some shoes, and I think a box of shotgun shells. So my
daddy set him a trap. He got one of the other niggers to
sleep in the store, and that night they caught this nigger
name of Richard. He was Dora's oldest boy, I guess no
older than you. How old are you?"

Toler told him.

"Not that old," Mr. Joe said. "I guess maybe nineteen or

twenty. And you know what my daddy did? He got two of the niggers on the place to hold him and he put the whip to him. Stretched him out on the floor in the back of that commissary, buck naked, and laid that strap across his back until he begged my daddy . . ." Mr. Joe looked through the windshield at the street, wet under the street lights, and down the street to the hazy outline of the monument. He could still, after all these years, see that nigger boy lying there, and he could hear that boy begging, and then he could feel the tears come in his eyes. He was twelve, or maybe thirteen, but he cried, just blubbered like a idiot, and his daddy heard him and said, *You cryin' over a nigger?* "But the point is," Mr. Joe said, "that nigger didn't steal again."

What is it? Toler thought. Where did it begin? With the first nigger they brought here? Or the first nigger to kill a white man? Some nigger must have killed some white man. And through the windshield, down the street, he saw the monument. When he was a boy he had climbed up on the monument—not that one but another one like it, in another Mississippi town. It was always the same soldier. Or, at least, they looked the same. Not like General Forrest looked. Or General Lee. Not like any soldier looked. And there was something written there: NEVER WAS A CAUSE SO JUST. Once he asked his mother that. *What was our cause?* And she asked him whose cause. *The cause,* he said, *that's written on the monument. What does it say?* she said. And he told her. *Well, it was to keep the slaves,* she said. *The Southerners wanted to keep their nigger slaves. . . .* It always comes back to that, he thought, eventually.

"Look yonder," said Mr. Joe.

It was a car. Toler saw the headlights and he saw the old man sit up in the seat, and he sat up, ready to turn the motor on. But the car passed, and it was a Plymouth coupé and there was a white man driving it. I'm just as glad, he thought.

Mr. Joe leaned back in his seat. Nine more days, he thought. Nine more days and these niggers better watch out, because this boy . . . "For a minute there," he said, and he laughed, "I thought we had us one."

At a quarter to four the northbound train came through, and they left their watch to cross the tracks to the depot. Mr. Joe used to meet that train and help the ladies with their things and, if there was no one there to meet them, drive them to their homes—sometimes as far as Gunnison. Tonight nobody got off and nobody got on. Mr. Joe stood there and talked to the flagman, and then the flagman waved his light and the engineer answered with a whistle and the train pulled out, headed north to Memphis.

"It won't be long," Mr. Joe said, "they'll do away with Number 12."

Toler looked down the tracks. "That train?"

"Yes, sir," Mr. Joe said. "That used to be the best train in the Delta. Everybody rode that train, because it put 'em in Memphis early enough to go about their business. Now," he said, and he got back in the car, "nobody rides it but the niggers."

Niggers, Toler thought: that's all he thinks about.

"Speaking of niggers," Mr. Joe said, when they had taken up their watch again, "reminds me of Charley Hubbard. You ever heard of Charley Hubbard?"

Toler shook his head.

"Charley Hubbard was a nigger who lived out here on Miss Eva Reynolds' place. Out around Beulah. He got sent up to Parchman for killing another nigger. I don't remember what it was about now. Anyhow," Mr. Joe said, "they made him a trusty and he was working as a houseboy for the warden or the assistant warden or one of the other officials. And the warden, or whoever it was, had a young daughter.

One Sunday morning Charley Hubbard pulled a knife on the warden, cut his throat from ear to ear, and took his daughter off with him. You can imagine all the hurrah. The girl was missing, and she turned up a day or so later in an abandoned nigger house. I don't think he had bothered her. Some said he did, some said he didn't; I never heard the straight of it. Anyhow," Mr. Joe said, "Charley Hubbard was loose and the whole state was looking for him. Bill Ellzey was the marshal then. Ellzey's uncle." And he thought: Bill Ellzey never would've let me go. That was the difference in a man like Tom McLean and a man like Bill Ellzey. "One morning we got word that Charley Hubbard had turned up on Miss Eva Reynolds' place, and that she was bringing him in herself, which might sound funny unless you knew Miss Eva. Oh, Miss Eva could do it. She had put that nigger in the back seat of her car and she was headed for the county jail. Only the mob got wind of it. They were out to get him, you know. I was there when they stopped her. She was going lickety-split down that gravel road, right there at the bend before you come into town, when the mob blocked the road ahead of her. She tried to turn around, and if it hadn't rained I guess she'd have got away, made it to Memphis. Miss Eva was quite a driver. But they stopped her. *Get out of my way and let me pass,* she said, *I'm taking this boy to Cleveland.* They didn't say anything. Bill Ellzey says, *Boys, let Miss Eva pass.* But they wouldn't listen to him. They just took that boy from her, and let her go, although there was some talk later about a white lady trying to help a nigger." For a minute Mr. Joe sat there, remembering how he had stood there that morning on the road. Bill Ellzey was right, he thought. There was nothing we could do. And it saved the state. The state would've had to bring the boy to trial, and it would've cost . . .

"What happened?" Toler said.

"That night," said Mr. Joe, "up near Rome, they burned Charley Hubbard. I guess half the state was at the burning. They had rode Charley Hubbard around all day, to give the governor time to leave the state, and there was time to get to the burning. I went up there myself. Just to see, you know. It was after dark when they set the torch to him, and everybody had turned their car lights on. There he was, in the circle of those headlights. And he spit on the white man who put the torch to him. Everybody remembers that: he spit on the white man who put the torch to him. But the point is . . ." Mr. Joe felt the pain. "The point is . . ." The smell came back to him, that burnt smell, and he remembered how sick he got. He got so sick he had to throw up, there on the road from Rome. What was the point? he thought. He forgot what the point was.

Toler laughed. He didn't know why, but he laughed.

If this boy had been there, Mr. Joe thought, he'd have been the one to set the torch to him. I never could have. I went up there to Rome to see him burn, but so did everybody else.

And Toler thought: I bet you were the one who put the torch to him. This old man hates niggers, he thought. He'd kill a nigger as soon as look at him.

Mr. Joe felt sick inside. I expect I got cancer, he thought. That pain again. You get old and that cancer you had for thirty years and didn't know about, or only said was gas, eats away at you. "What time is it?" he said.

It was close to four thirty.

"I think I'll get me a little shut-eye. If you see anything that looks like a carload of niggers . . ." Mr. Joe slumped down in the seat. I wonder what he thinks, he thought. It ain't that I don't like niggers, because I do: I could tell stories about how much I like niggers. "It's a funny thing

. . ." he said. "My mama used to tell me this. When I was a baby . . . that was before they had milk like they do now . . . my mama went dry. And they could've give me cow's milk, but in those days . . . you know, a mother's milk and all. And Dora . . . she was Mama's nigger woman . . ." He closed his eyes and saw Dora's face. "She had William Vick about the same time. She was nursing him, you know, and she had plenty of milk." Mr. Joe laughed. "So Mama got her to nurse me too. And when I was a boy, my daddy would josh me. He'd say, *You was raised on nigger milk, don't that make you part nigger?* And I used to ask my mama if I was. It worried me, you know. I wonder how many white men's been nursed by a nigger. . . ."

I wonder, Toler thought.

"So you see . . ."

For a long time after the old man was quiet Toler sat there looking out into the night. He thought of the old man and he thought of the only nigger he had known, because he had never known that nigger sergeant, or any of the rest of them, but that cook named Bea he had. If he had never smelled that house . . . but that smell was a smell that hung to him. Once, just after five o'clock, he saw a car come down the street and when the car passed under the street light he saw that it was a Buick and that a nigger man was driving it. And he sat there and let it pass, its lights upon the monument.

The old man heard the car. He was thinking of Tom McLean, of that day he and Tom McLean drove over to the bluehole and caught all those fish and the snake got in the boat and Tom jumped overboard. And just as he was laughing to himself, he heard the car. I hope it's not, he thought. And if it is, I hope the boy's asleep. So the car passed. After a while he opened his eyes and saw that the boy was still awake, or had come awake, and he said, "I guess I must've slept."

"Yeah," Toler said.

"No niggers?"

"No niggers," Toler said.

The watch ended at six. The whistle at the oil mill blew. It was daylight by then and the streets were still wet, and when they passed the monument Toler saw that someone had taken a piece of chalk and scrawled across the base of it: THE SOUTH WILL RISE AGAIN. The soldier did not see it. He looked straight ahead, beyond the water tank and the street of stores and the road where Miss Eva Reynolds was stopped when she tried to save a nigger.

When they got back to the city hall, Tom McLean had already come on. "How'd it go, Joe?" he said.

Mr. Joe said, "Quiet."

"That's good. Won't be long and you'll be in your bed at night like a white man ought to, and Toler here . . ." Tom McLean laughed. "How you going to like it, boy?"

"Long as I can sleep in the mornings," Toler said.

"But that night shift gets old. Don't it, Joe? When Toler here's coming off at six and I'm going on, you're going to laugh at us." Tom McLean looked at him. "How about us running over to the café for a cup of coffee? I'm buying the coffee."

Toler said, "Thank you, Mr. Tom, but I expect I better head on home. . . ." He was thinking of Wilda, lying there in bed asleep, and of how tired he was. But not *that* tired, he thought: you don't get *that* tired.

"I'll take you up on that coffee," Mr. Joe said. Tom McLean had bought him a cup of coffee every morning since he put him on the night shift. Maybe that was why. They would sit there in the café and Tom would say, *It gets harder and harder* . . . He meant, *to get up.* And maybe, Mr. Joe thought, *to go on living.*

They went out on the wet street.

"See you tonight, Mr. Joe," Toler said.

"Yeah," Mr. Joe said. "Tonight . . ." Tonight, he thought, there are lots of stories I could tell, about what a friend I been to niggers, what a friend they been to me. Like the time old Dora was about to die and she said she wanted to see her church just one more time, I took her there. I put her in the front seat next to me and we drove out there to that country church. Oh, there are stories and stories. But you can't tell *them.* Not to this boy. You can't tell *them.*

There was a wind out of the north. Mr. Joe sniffed it and thought of that night, there on the road from Rome. Then he remembered what the point was: it was an awful thing, but you can't have that; you've got to show 'em . . .

Toler sniffed the same wind, and smelled a house. He wondered if drinking a nigger's milk made a man part nigger. Or eating a nigger's pie. Or (and this was the point, he thought) being spit on by a nigger when you tried to put the torch to him.

Journey
to the
Pyramids

They had been riding all day. They had left Springfield before daylight and by noon had passed Memphis and were headed south and the excitement was beginning to mount in Leggett. "Shit," he said, "I remember these towns." It was all coming back to him, and not only these towns or the camp that he was looking for but a time when he was more alive than he would ever be again. "We finished our basic and we came through here on a troop train," he said, "and all the girls were down to the station to see us." Leggett kept his eyes on the road, but for a moment he was on the troop train again, bare to the waist, leaning out of the door, and the wind was in his face and the smell of train smoke

in his nose. Pearson and Federoff and Metcalf were there
by him and he could smell their sweat, and Metcalf was
singing, *Hidy didy, christamighty, who the hell are we?*
Pearson too. *Zim zam, goddam, we're the infantry* . . . And
Federoff said, *Knock it off, we're coming into a town.* Then
they were passing through the town and the girls were
there beside the tracks and the old men who had come out
of the pool hall were waving, too, and Leggett thought:
There'll never be a time like this. He took the piece of paper
out of his pocket and saw it flutter in the wind and swoop
almost under the train and out again, and there were other
pieces of paper in that wind, and the girls were reaching for
them. One of them would sit down and write in a very careful hand, *Dear Pvt. Leggett, I got your name and address
you threw off the train* . . . And she would send him a picture, and he would send her a picture, one of those pictures
he had taken in Omaha with his cap off, that showed his hair
cut short and his sunburnt face, better-looking than he was,
and they would write again and maybe never see each other
unless he could get there on a weekend pass. Then he would
take her a bottle of Chanel No. 5 from the PX and she would
ask him to her house, and he would meet her folks, and they
would sit there in the living room and talk. Later he would
take her to the picture show, to the last row in the balcony,
or sometimes to a dance, and if he thought she might he
would put the make to her, take her outside, out behind the
gym or the Legion hall or armory, or to somebody's car, because a girl liked to get laid in the back seat of a car, or on
her own front porch, if you talked her into it. Sometimes
when Leggett thought about the war he thought about all
those soldiers on all those front porches.

"You sure you know where you're going?" Lois said.

"Hell, yes, I know where I'm going," he said.

But toward late afternoon the towns were smaller and

farther apart and he stopped and pulled off on the side of the road to look at a map. He had had to detour and he had taken the wrong turn in a town and now he was on the blacktop road that he remembered led up past the camp.

"I don't know what you wanted to come way off down here for," she said, and she reached over the back of the seat into the cooler and opened him another beer.

"You didn't have to come," he said.

"I know I didn't." She drank a swallow of the beer and handed it to him. "Six hundred miles to see a army camp. You must be crazy or something."

Leggett put the can to his mouth and tasted the beer and he thought of the night he and Metcalf chugalugged beer until they staggered out of the beer joint and down the road and into a field, to shake the dew off, and they fell down in the field and laughed, and Metcalf said, *When this is over . . . Christ.* Maybe that was why they laughed. They were there in that field and they could hear the music from the beer joint and the sound of a convoy on the road, and they knew that it would never be over.

Lois said, "What you going to do when you get there? Turn around?"

"For Christ's sake," he said, and he thought: How you going to tell her? She wasn't old enough. She wasn't even on the front porch with one of the others. It was all so long ago, and nothing had happened since. That was the trouble. He had come back from the war to a job he didn't want, to a town he didn't like, to a life like everybody else's. People were born and people died, but nothing happened. So he went back to work at the plant and he joined the VFW and nearly married a girl who had been married to a Marine lieutenant killed on Saipan, but she didn't know what she wanted and he didn't either. Then that summer he met Lois at a skating rink. She was just a kid, not even very pretty, but fun to be with. She reminded him of the girls he had known in the Army. The first thing he knew he was asking her to marry him. Maybe he thought that would change things. It didn't. Once in a while they would go back to the skating rink, or bowl, or he would take her to the picture show and they would sit up in the balcony, but they always came home, and when he tried to tell her he couldn't. If I could tell her, he thought: what it was like. But she wouldn't understand. So he tried not to think about it. Even when he was knocking off a piece he tried not to think about it. *What's the matter?* she'd say. And he'd say, *Nothing,* trying to think of something else.

"I checked the speedometer," Leggett said. "It ought to be right about here."

But when they crossed the hill there was nothing there except the blacktop road and the green fields on either side and a straggly growth of yaupon and briers.

"I would've swore it was right about here," he said. He saw Lois look at him. "It couldn't be much farther."

"I hope you're not getting us lost," she said.

Women, he thought, they can piss you off, and he drove on in silence, faster now, across a hill and another.

"When was that?" she said.

"What you mean?" He turned and looked at her.

"When you were here."

" 'Forty-four," he said.

" 'Forty-four," she said, and laughed.

"What's so funny?"

"Nothing," she said.

"Then what were you laughing at?"

"Oh," she said, "I was just thinking: you should've stayed in the Army."

I sure as hell should have, he thought.

There was a house at the top of the next hill. As they drew

nearer Leggett saw that it was one of those big unpainted frame houses that he had seen so often in the South. There was an old man sitting on the porch.

"There's a house," Lois said. "Why don't you ask?"

He began to slow the car and when he reached the turn-off pulled up in the yard and got out.

The old man left his chair and walked to the steps. "Good evening," he said.

"Good evening," Leggett said. "I was looking for the camp . . ."

The old man stared at him.

"I thought the camp was right about here."

"Van Dorn?"

Leggett nodded.

"Back there," the old man said. He pointed. "A couple of miles back. What's left of it."

Leggett looked at him.

"You must've been stationed at Van Dorn."

"In 'forty-four," he said.

"There was many a boy there," the old man said. He said it with a kind of sadness, and Leggett thought: He knows; he wasn't in the war, but he knows. "You might want to go back and have a look. The Government sold the land for pasturage. All the buildings are gone. There's a water tank . . ."

"How long has it been?"

"Oh," the old man said, "not long after the war."

All this time, Leggett thought. He thanked the man and went back to the car.

"Well," Lois said, "what did he say?"

"We passed it."

"Passed it?"

"There's nothing there."

"You mean . . . ?"

"How the hell did I know?" he said.

Leggett turned around and drove back down the blacktop road. He was thinking: I've come all this way and there's nothing there, just a lot of land for pasturage. But he felt it still—the excitement. Like the time he saw Metcalf. He hadn't seen Metcalf since the war and when he sat there in that café in Cleveland, waiting for Metcalf, he kept wondering what it would be like, what they would say. He would say, *You remember the chaplain's wine?* And he did, and Metcalf said, *Boy, you don't forget anything, do you?* Like he was ashamed of stealing that bottle of Communion wine. Only he wasn't ashamed at the time, and over there, in one of those clumps of woods on the side of one of those hills, they drank the wine, he and Metcalf and a boy from Kansas who'd never had his first piece, and broke the bottle on a tree.

"That must be where it was," Lois said.

Leggett slowed the car. Between the trees, half a mile or more away, he could see the water tank. Then he could see, scattered on the ground among the yaupon bushes, the concrete foundations on which the buildings had stood.

"No wonder we missed it," Lois said.

"The main gate used to be here," he said. He pulled off on the shoulder of the road.

"You going to stop?" Lois said. But he was already out of the car. "I'll wait here."

"The hell you will," he said. "You going to come with me . . ."

"Leggett . . ."

"You don't understand, do you?"

"What?" she said.

"What it was like," he said. "I was here, Lois." He remembered how they rode through this gate and how the German POW's looked up from their work to stare at them and how it smelled, the pine trees and the wind up from the Gulf—like it smelled now. "Open me another beer," he said.

She handed it to him through the window.

"Get out," he said. "I want to show you where my barracks was."

"Leggett," she said, "let me wait here in the car. There's briers. They'll tear my stockings."

"Take your goddam stockings off," he said, and he thought: Women, for Christ's sake, they know how to chap your ass.

Lois got out of the car. He helped her under the barbed wire fence and lay on the ground and rolled under himself and came up on the other side.

"There's some cows over there," she said.

"They won't hurt you," he said.

They made their way around a tangle of vines and came to a strip of blacktop almost overgrown with grass. "This used to be one of the streets," Leggett said, the excitement in his voice. "There was a PX down that hill . . ." He pointed. "And over yonder . . . a little to the right of those cows, was the chapel. . . ."

"You mean the church?" she said.

"Yeah," he said, "the church. One time they put Metcalf on the chaplain's work detail. They had caught him answering muster for one of the boys in the company. You know what he did? Slipped the key to the place where the chaplain kept the wine. Stole a bottle, and me and another boy helped him drink it."

"You mean you drank the Communion wine?"

"Hell, yes." Leggett laughed. "Another time," he said, "me and Metcalf figured we had a little leave coming. So we waited until after bed-check and went over the hill. Hitch-hiked a ride back into town. There were some girls in town . . ."

"What kind of girls?"

"Aw, some pigs," Leggett said. "But there was a war on. You couldn't afford to be choosy."

"No telling what you did with those girls," Lois said.

Leggett smiled. I sure as hell ain't telling, he thought.

"Well," Lois said, "you've seen what used to be the camp. You ready to go back?"

"Hell, no," he said. "I told you I wanted to show you where our barracks was. First Platoon, Charlie Company."

"How you going to know where your barracks was?"

"You follow me," he said.

They walked up the blacktop street past a herd of grazing cows and crossed the field to another strip of blacktop which ended in a stand of pines. On either side of them, out there in the weeds and briers, were little pyramids of concrete, where the barracks had once stood.

"You see over yonder?" Leggett said. "You see that ditch?"

Lois nodded.

"That used to be the obstacle course. You had to jump the ditch, and there was a wall and some pipe and a lot of other crap. Once they made Metcalf run it three times. They didn't think he could." Leggett remembered Metcalf's face. He had made it around the third time and he was lying on the ground and the sergeant was standing over him, maybe wondering if he'd run his guts out, and Metcalf saw him and kind of smiled, as if to say, *Screw you.* And Leggett remembered how he had waited in that café in Cleveland. He hadn't seen Metcalf since the war and he was passing through and decided to give him a ring. Christ, he thought, it'll be just like the old days. But it wasn't. Metcalf might as well have been a stranger. Oh, they talked about the Army days, but it was Leggett who did most of the talking. Metcalf just sat there, as if it didn't matter. He pulled out pictures of his wife and kids (he had three kids, one of them a sissy-looking boy with glasses Leggett never would have thought was Metcalf's kid) and he asked Leggett how many kids he had and when Leggett told him none, he said, *You ought to*. And Leggett laughed and said, *Yeah, I'm trying*. But trying ain't enough, he thought.

"The sun's going to be going down soon," Lois said. "I think we ought to head back." They had crossed one of the hills and the road and the car were out of sight.

"Not until I show you my barracks," Leggett said. "It's over that way . . ."

"I'm going back to the car," she said.

"No, you ain't," he said, and he headed across the field and through a clump of yaupon toward a row of concrete foundations on the other side. He could almost see the barracks and he could smell the barracks smell: sweat and soap and shoe polish and leather and pine lumber, and always the men who had been there earlier. Sometimes, lying awake in his bunk at night, Leggett would wonder who they were, the ones who had been there and moved on and who would follow after him. Jew-boys from the Bronx and Swedes from Minnesota and Texans, mountaineers, men from the plains, plowboys and wanderers.

"Leggett . . ."

He stopped to drink a swallow of the beer and he heard Lois calling him.

"You about to walk me to death."

"Come on over here," he said. He was thinking of Metcalf. I wonder what happened? he thought. Metcalf made it through the war and he went back home to Cleveland and married the most pisspoor girl he could find and got him a job working for the post office and had three sickly-looking kids and all he thought about was showing their pictures. Christ, the post office, Leggett thought.

"Is this it?" she said.

"It's one of these along here," he said. He picked up a

stick and beat at a patch of weeds between the rows of concrete pyramids.

"What you doing?" she said.

"Looking," he said.

"What for?"

"I'll show you," he said, and he ran across the field to the
next row of foundations, hopping over them.

"You going to fall down and break your crazy neck," she
said.

"This must've been the mess hall." Leggett stood among
the foundations, looking at the ground.

"You better hurry up," Lois called. "It's going to be dark
before long."

He turned and looked across the field toward the road and
the sun that was setting in the west. Down the hill the cows
were grazing. To his right he could see the water tank—all
that was left. A water tank and some blacktop streets that
went nowhere and these rows of concrete foundations, like
graves. Suddenly he was sad, because time had passed and
because Metcalf had changed and because nothing was now
this real to him. Not Lois. Not the plant where he worked.
Not the bowling alley where he went on Tuesday nights, or
anything his television set could bring him. Nothing was this
real. He drank the rest of the beer and threw the can—as far
as he could; it sailed across the blacktop street where the
Old Man used to drive his jeep, out toward the field where
the company used to drill.

"I'm going back, Leggett," Lois called.

"No, you ain't," he said. Now, frantically, as if to prove
that what he knew was true, he began to run among the
concrete pyramids, beating the bushes away, peering at the
ground. He was laughing, and when he found what he was
looking for he was still laughing. "You see?" he said.

She came across the field toward him, very slowly, and

without a word she knelt down and saw in the brown earth in front of four concrete pyramids what two boys, a thousand years before, had written there.

"Me and Metcalf," he said, "we put it there." There in the white shells they had spelled out 1st PLATOON, C COMPANY. Leggett could read it still. "This was our barracks," he said.

"Now we can go," Lois said. It was almost dark. The sun had dropped behind the trees on the far horizon and the bats had begun to circle in the summer sky.

Leggett sat down on one of the concrete pyramids. "Sit down here," he said.

She sat down there.

"I wish I could tell you," he said. "It was like . . ." He picked up one of the white shells. "Everything that was going to happen happened . . ."

Long after Lois had gotten up and gone down across the field and over the hill to the road and the car, Leggett sat there. He watched the moon come up and he heard a plane pass overhead and once off in the direction of the road he thought he heard Lois calling him. He knew that one minute soon he would get up and go the way that she had gone, back into a life in which nothing happened—and nothing would.